Getting Across

T.M. Duncan

Contents

Prologue..1

Chapter 1..3

Chapter 2..16

Chapter 3..31

Chapter 4..44

Chapter 5..57

Chapter 6..74

Chapter 7..85

Chapter 8..94

Chapter 9..103

Chapter 10..117

Chapter 11..126

Chapter 12..137

Chapter 13..145

Chapter 14..160

Chapter 15..171

Chapter 16..180

Chapter 17..190

Epilogue...201

Prologue

I realized that I was getting old after eating a banana down to the soft, brown spot that I'd always avoided. I paused, poked at the brown mush, shrugged, and kept right on eating. Grandma, who we called Maman, had always claimed that it was the sweet spot.

After that, it seemed all the other signs of aging webbed out of hiding. There were the grays around my temples and a few more that covered God's glory— the triangle between my hips. There were the wrinkles around my eyes whenever I smiled and my breasts weren't as "excited" as they used to be. I couldn't stand as quickly and my bones ached as the seasons changed.

Maman would say this the time to "make it right" before it got to be too late. Lord knows that I had plenty rounds to make, beginning with the five girls that I laid down and pushed out. Maman told me a long time ago, in her back room—the same room that she used wire hangers to scrape seeds out of wombs, sold jars of herbal healings out of, and read people's future—that I would eventually bore five girls. I didn't believe it then and didn't think nothing else about it until now. I guess I was living too fast to think about it back then.

Now that I'm up in age, I can only pray that they found it in their own hearts to understand my decision. Pamela, my youngest, had only been two when I left, so she wouldn't have known the difference anyway. It was the other four—Doris, Reta, Mona, and

1

Annette—that I was concerned about. If nothing else, hopefully I showed them that when it's your time to go, you don't question it. You just pick up one or two things and go. You can't let things other folk say you can't do hold you back. Otherwise you'll die old and wretched. I would proudly choose dying young and happy over the latter.

"Turn over for me, Ms. Louisa."

"Gimme a second child. I can't move like I used to," I said, grabbing ahold of the cold metal bar on the other side of the bed. You'd think we'd get something a lil' more comfortable for all the money we paid.

"You wrote that letter to your girls yet?"

"Not 'chet. Not 'chet. What you 'spose I put in the letter?"

"Well you could start off with saying you sorry."

"I don' tried that already."

"When was that?"

"Lemme think. What year is this here?"

"95," she answered.

"Well not too long ago. 'Bout ten, fifteen years ago, I reckon."

"Did they write back at least?"

I chuckled. "Well my oldest girl, Doris, wrote me back. She said that I made my bed and to lay in it. She said too that I bet not bring my black ass back to New Orleans."

2

Chapter 1

W alter, better known as Trouble Man, had been my ticket out of Coushatta. Just as I had begun to shrug away my hopes of ever leaving, he came along. I met him by way of my friend Girly who was from North Carolina. She ain't grow up in Coushatta like the rest of us. When Maman died, it messed me up in a way that I didn't expect. I had quit going to school against everyone's wishes, figuring it made no sense. The only woman I knew to actually use her education was my teacher, Sister Clare. Other than that, every other woman I knew either cleaned up after white folks, cleaned up after their husbands and kids, or both.

Girly's mama had passed and she was shipped down to Louisiana. Like me, she never knew her daddy. So she had to move in with her aunt, Miss Eula Mae. Miss Eula Mae had six kids of her own—all boys. Trouble Man, the oldest, had left to go to war. If you ask me, he probably waged war as more comfortable than being packed in that cramped, two-bedroom house with five other niggas. I never understood how they worked out those living arrangements.

Girly never complained. Hell, she even did it with some of her cousins. That was her favorite pastime, *doing it*. She, too, had quit school, but she wasn't the brightest, so I'm sure no one even second guessed her decision. She was bound to wound up with a houseful of kids with different daddies. That's something I foresaw even as a child. I never bothered her about doing it with her cousins or down talked her because she was my friend.

Our hangout spot was a raggedy little red dwelling behind the church that had been abandoned. Weeds drawled around the barn in a way to where you had to kind of rush the door to open it. Nobody ever tended to it or went back there, so that made it the perfect spot. Frank and Eugene were two of the other five cousins who Girly lived with. Frank was handsome. Short, stout, with squared shoulders, but everything was proportionate. That's who Girly messed with. Eugene, on the other hand…not so much. And on top of that, he stuttered. I tolerated it because he was just a boy toy to me. I couldn't say the same for him though. The boy was head over heels for me.

When we went to the barn, we either smoked cigarettes—I would only pretend to though or watch the boys roll dice. Girly and Frank were the main ones doing it. I guess you could say that Eugene and I were just experimenting. I was practicing for when my real boyfriend came along. Eugene didn't know that though. He really didn't know much at all: nothing about my body, his, or what they were supposed to do when they got together. So I did all the work. I was in control and liked it that way.

By my thirteenth birthday, I decided that it was time to go all the way. It fell on a Sunday and I had already begun to hate church as is, so I ain't plan on spending my whole day there. Damn that. Eugene and I agreed to meet in the barn about an hour after service started. Sister Nadine would have caught the Holy Ghost by then which would have refueled Rev and bought us some time to do what we needed to do.

"Gawd said, 'Call upon me in the day of your troubles and I will deliver you.'" The church clapped and shouted at Rev's third-time-in-a-row sermon. "He ain't say call on mama. He ain't say call on daddy. He ain't say call Jezebel. Y'all don' got quiet now," he said, chuckling. I swear the man amused himself more than anybody else I knew.

"Sister Turner read to 'em the fiftieth chapter of Psalms verse fifteen."

I finally figured out that although Rev knew the bible backwards and forwards and inside and out, he didn't know how to read. So he always called on Sister Turner, who could flip to a scripture faster than Rev could say it. I just wished she could read as fast.

"Call…upon…me…in—"

"—Stop right there! What does it say church? Call upon who?"

"ME!" shouted the church as they had for the past two Sundays.

"Go on Sister Turner."

"Your…day…of…trouble…I…will—"

"—Stop right there!"

I slid down in my seat and put my bible over my face. Mama pinched me, which only pissed me off even more. My sister Etta rolled her eyes at me. Mama, with her right arm stretched across the back of Etta's seat, saw her do it, but what did she do? She smiled and crossed her left leg over her right, kicking me further out the picture. I didn't care though. Caring didn't change anything and crying surely didn't. Mama hated when I cried. She said that I was being weak and sorry like my daddy. Me and Etta were twins—fraternal, but twins nonetheless—so I never understood why he was always "my daddy" instead of "our daddy." From what the ladies in the church say, Mama didn't know who our daddy was.

When I was sure that Mama wasn't looking, I rolled my eyes back at Etta and her ugly face. I hated her because I hated our mama and she tried her damnest to act and look just like our mama. Mama wasn't anybody to be trying to be like. Even as a child, I knew that. She talked behind people's backs and smiled in their face. She lied about everything and would eat white people's shit if they let her. I hated her.

I looked over and saw Deacon Russell standing against the wall, staring at me. When he caught my eye, he winked. *Ugh.* He had a way of making me feel filthy just from looking at me. Like he could see straight through my clothes and inside my head. What made it worse is that he knew I didn't like him, but messed with me still. I looked straight ahead, pretending to be interested in the sermon, but he was still staring at me. I could feel it. Since I wasn't going to be there for the whole sermon, I dealt with it.

Soon, Rev started pacing, sweating, and moaning. Sister Nadine had begun shouting and dancing. I held my breath, but didn't realize it until she collapsed and I let my breath out. The deaconess rushed to cover her skirt with a kerchief and fan her. I held up my index finger and excused myself from the building. Eugene jumped out of nowhere grinning with those big, ugly, pink lips spread across his face. I pushed him in the barn, afraid that someone would spot us, and accuse me of being fast. It had happened before and I denied it. If it happened again, there wouldn't no way I'd talk myself out of it a second time. Prime reason I couldn't wait to move out of that country town.

Eugene handed me some flowers that he'd picked out of from in front of the city hall. They were the prettiest flowers that I had ever seen and the most special gift that I ever received—even with the dirty roots still attached. I was always tempted to snatch one, but my nerves got the best of me every time. It was a rumor that two Black men were hung right outside the front just for looking at the building too hard. Wasn't certain if it was true or not, but I wasn't about to gamble it. Since Eugene went out of his way for me, I was actually going to meet him halfway this time. I was going to go all the way with him. Or at least I thought I was.

We covered the window with stacks of hay to block the sun. Sunlight speckled through the red planks and from under the door.

Eugene covered one of the splintered benches with his shirt and I lay down and propped my legs up. He stood there smiling like a prisoner on a conjugal visit. I told him to pull his pants down, which he did without hesitation. He walked over and stood between my legs waiting on the next instruction. Big dummy.

"Sit down," I said, pointing. He did. Like a damn dog. Whatever I said, he did. No questions asked. Sometimes I liked it. Other times, it was annoying. I wiggled my stockings down, put his hand between my legs and then pushed his finger inside of me. He flashed his big, stupid grin and I wished that we could've made the room a little darker. Since that was impossible, I did the next best thing which was to close my eyes. I imagined him to be one of his fine brothers. I threw my head back between my shoulder blades and enjoyed my moment. It wasn't me and Eugene. It was me and Trouble Man. Still in his uniform. It started feeling good, which made me feel like a woman. Doing what I wanted to do, with who I wanted to do it with.

Then the door creaked open.

We shot straight up. My breath jammed in the middle of my chest. Eugene pulled his pants back up and I yanked my dress back down, but was caught pulling my stockings back up. We were caught. The sunlight plus the caul of shame that covered our faces made it difficult to see.

"What's going on in here?" boomed Deacon Russell. His eyes switched back and forth from me to Eugene.

"What's yo' name boy?" he asked the way daddies do when they find out about their princesses' boyfriend.

"Eugene B-b-brown, sir."

"Brown," Deacon Russell repeated slowly. "You one of Tootsie's boys?"

"N-n-no sir. Eula Mae, sir."

7

"That's right. That's right. Sho'llnuff. Whatchu thank she'll have to say 'bout dis?"

Eugene's head bobbed like a chicken while he struggled to make out his response. He couldn't get it out, so Deacon said it for him. "She wouldn't be too happy 'bout dis now would she?"

Eugene shook his head with emphasis. "N-n-no sir."

"Well I'd advise you to gone on home."

"Louisa w-w-won't get in no tr-r-r-ouble, will she?"

Deacon stepped forward with his chest out. "You testing me boy?"

"No sir. N-n-no disrespect meant. Just ain't want Louisa taking the fall for my blame."

Deacon Russell stepped to the side and opened the door. Eugene looked at me. His eyes apologized a thousand times. I smiled to say thanks and that I'd be okay. Deacon Russell closed the door, leaving us alone in the barn. He stood there thumbing his suspenders, looking at me like he wanted to eat me. My bowels went to churning making my stomach hurt and feel heavy. I moved toward the door. He took one step to the side, blocking my exit. My heart crawled up in my throat and I wanted to cry, but didn't know why. I backed up slowly.

"I wanna go back to church now, Mr. Russell," I said in my smallest voice. I wished it came out louder and stronger, more like I was sure of myself, but the woman I was a few minutes ago had left with Eugene.

He walked toward me until he was standing right over me. I sat down before he knocked me down.

"Don't you know what young boys like that do to girls?" he asked. "Dem young boys don't mean you no good."

"We wasn't doing nothing, Mr. Russell."

"Who you thank you fooling, gal? I been young befo'."

He thumbed his suspenders faster. If he went any faster, he would strike a fire. The way he looked at me made me feel naked and small. I thought he would eat me for sure. I wanted to cry. I wanted to beg him to just let me out. I wanted to ask what he wanted from me. I wanted to scream. To just start flailing my arms and legs until somebody came for me. I should've, but I didn't.

"Take dem stockings off," he demanded, removing his belt.

My eyes widened and my tongue froze, not knowing which of the ten million questions I wanted to ask first. I should've asked the one that stuck out the most. Why did I have to take off my stockings for a spanking? I had never had a spanking before, but that couldn't have been necessary. They were thin enough. The wrong move would rip 'em, so surely I would get the same effect without taking 'em off.

He peeked through the red planks from two walls. Satisfied that no one was around, he again ordered me to take off my stockings. I couldn't move. I didn't want to move. I wanted to wake up and thank God that it was only a dream. I wanted to turn the time back and stay my ass in church. I wanted Eugene to change his mind and come back for me.

"Either I learn you a lesson now or I'll make you go in front that church and confess yo' sin befo' dem. I'm sho' Maureen won't like that very much. Marie ain't here no more to stop her."

Again, I couldn't speak. I wanted to say too many things. I wanted to tell him that he used learn when he should've used teach, but I wasn't in the position to be correcting nobody. I wanted to ask him what sin I had committed and I wanted to know how much he knew about my family's business.

"Matta fact, take off the dress. Since you wanna be fast, I'ma give you what you been itching fo'."

I bubbled over in tears and snot. He shushed me and made me move faster. I swiped the mess on my face with one elbow-to-wrist motion hoping that he'd either pity me or be disgusted.

9

Neither happened. I think it did the opposite, because he went to unbuckling his pants real fast and breathing real heavy.

One leg after the other, I stepped out of my stockings. One button at a time, I unfastened my dress. A thunderous roar of claps and praises rang out from the church. I wanted so bad to be in there. I didn't care if it was Rev's one hundredth time preaching that sermon. I recalled the scripture, Psalms 50:15. I prayed like the right amount of words would make the sky crack open. I was in trouble and I needed deliverance. I closed my eyes and prayed harder. I opened my eyes wishing for a miracle, but instead saw Deacon Russell patting his lap. I cried harder.

"Hush, gal."

I shouldn't have hushed. I should've cried louder. I should've screamed, but instead I muffled my cries in my dress that I'd balled up in my hand. He ran one of his fingers from the top of my butt to my private. He tried to wrestle my legs open, while I wiggled to keep them closed. I begged for him to stop, but I don't even think he heard me. He was too hungry. My tiny body was no match for his. I gave up. Why did Maman have to die and why didn't God save me? I felt my private tearing and I began falling into a cache of darkness where I couldn't see anything. I couldn't hear anything and I almost couldn't feel anything until Deacon Russell shook the hell out of me. Blink by blink, I was back in the barn.

He handed me my dress. "Now I bet you'll thank twice 'bout tryna be so fast," he said, buckling his pants.

I didn't answer. I was choked with shame, guilt, disgust, and regret. Blood stained the insides of my sticky thighs and my private felt like someone had butchered it and poured alcohol on the wound. I reached down to touch it and there was more blood. It burned and felt nasty. I wanted to leave it right there in the barn, but I couldn't, because unfortunately, it was a part of me.

Girly was the only one who I'd told what had happened. I expected her to be disgusted, or at the least, tell me that I needed to tell a grownup. I wanted her, no, I needed her, to tell me that what Deacon did was wrong and that I did nothing wrong. She didn't. Instead, she threw her head back and laughed from the gut.

"Girl, what you cryin' fo? That happen to all women," she said with a flick of her wrist. She leaned in and lowered her voice. "Hell, you lucky he ain't take you and still tell yo' mama 'bout you and Eugene."

She was right. Or at least I figured that she had to be. She was my friend. She could've judged me, but she didn't. She could've lied to me, but she didn't. On top of that, she was older than me by three years, so I assumed that she knew more about the world. I lowered my head and shuffled the dirt with my foot, digesting yet another reality. Not only was I black which meant that I was bound to be poor forever. But I was also a woman, which meant that I had no rights to nothing, not even my body. It was up for grabs until I got married and even then, its right would be handed over to my husband. I kicked a pinecone that landed in my path.

"My daddy broke my virgin," she said.

"I thought you ain't know yo' daddy," I replied.

"Not my real daddy, stupid. My mama second husband."

"Oh."

"I fixed his ass though."

"How?" I asked.

"I started charging him."

The look I gave her must have asked all the questions mounting in my mind. Nodding her head, she added, "Yep. Taxed his ass. A quarter for every kiss, fifty cent if he wanted to go sticking his dick up in me, and a dollar for every time he wanted me to put my mouth on the nasty thing." Then she turned her head and looked at me grinning again. "And I'm talking a case dollar too, not no four quarters."

She extended her hand for a high five. I met her hand with mine, but only half smiled. Was that all that I was worth? A dollar? Sensing my gloom, she asked, "What's wrong witchu?"

I shrugged. "I don't know. It just don't seem fair."

She kicked a pine cone. "Life ain't never been fair to women. We the ones that got to bleed every month, just to be taken, then suffer for nine months only to really suffer during labor. Then raise the bastards while they go out and stick they johns in the next one. Ain't nothing fair about being a woman." She stopped and faced me. "Less you make it fair."

"How I'm s'posed to do that?" I asked.

"Do it to who-e-vah you want to," she said tilting her head from side to side with each syllable. "Your daddy, your cousin, your neighbor, your pastor. Hell, even the president if you want to." We both laughed. "Just make sho' you charge his ass."

Now I would be a lie to say that it didn't still bother me. I could still feel Deacon Russell's hands all over me and sometimes, I could even smell him. I threw away the dress, shoes, and stockings that I had been wearing. It didn't take long for mama to take notice that it was missing either. Since I couldn't give a good enough explanation as to what happened to them, she declared that I just wouldn't be getting nothing else. "Round here acting like money grow on trees. Always thank somebody owe yo' tail something. *Humph.* I'll show you. See if my good money go on yo tail again." Since I didn't wanna explain, I just dealt with the fact that she wasn't buying me anything else. So long as Girly's plans worked out right, then I wouldn't need mama to buy me nothing else anyhow.

Girly suggested that I start the plan off right away. So that's what I did. She said to go to church, smiling, and act like nothing ever happened. When I caught Deacon Russell's eye, I was to smile, and excuse myself. I didn't think that he would follow me out again. After all, he knew that what he did was wrong, so why would he risk getting caught all over again?

"Girl, do you know anythang? That nigga coming to that barn." She wide-eyed me, daring me to doubt her. "I gua-ran-tee it!"

"What if he take me again, but don't pay me?" My stomach churned at the thought of being in the barn alone again with Deacon Russell. His big, hungry eyes, heavy breathing, and dripping sweat. My still burned down there sometimes and it wasn't a second that I wasn't thinking about it. Even when I slept, I dreamed about it. How would I be able to do that again on purpose?

"Oh he'll pay you! He want your stuff just that bad. All men do! They don't care. If he threaten to tell yo' mama bout you and Eugene, then tell him that you'll tell about what he did."

I just couldn't see that working. Ain't no man in his right mind would do that again. I could have told somebody about what he did by now. Plus, ain't nobody would believe that he did that anyhow. Even if I did tell, which I could never do, they treated Deacon Russell like God's right hand man. He would just laugh in my face, take me again, and leave with my money and my dignity.

Reading my suspicions, she added. "Well if it suits you any, I'll be stooped in the woods behind the barn. Just holler and I'll come."

I never thought to ask her what she would do when she came. She was no bigger than I was. Or, how long she would be waiting? Or, what if he somehow stuffed my mouth and I couldn't holler? Like the mule I was, I got dressed Sunday morning not knowing what to expect. Deacon Russell stared me damn near the whole service, just like Girly said he would.

I figured that I'd wait long enough for Girly to be in them woods, but not too long for her to leave. Rev was on the same sermon that he preached on my birthday last week, the week before that, and the one before that one too. I waited for the Holy Ghost to visit Sister Nadine and like clockwork, He came knocking. She went to jumping, shouting, and losing shoes. I peeked over at Deacon Russell, who happened to be looking at me too. Against my heart's wishes, I smiled, and slipped up my index finger.

I struggled to get one leg after the other to make it to the barn. I felt that at any moment they would defy me and give out. I needed my body to cooperate if this was going to work. My arms felt like bricks, weighing me down. I stroked them, assuring them that it was going to be okay. They replied with goose bumps. I quickly scanned the wood line looking for my friend. Although I didn't see her, I trusted that she was there. I figured that she was just hiding real good so as not to blow the plan. Plus, she was my friend, so I knew she wouldn't leave me when I needed her most. I pushed the door open with my shoulder, leaving it cracked just a bit. I didn't want Deacon Russell just surprising me again. I had to at least see him coming.

Just as Girly said he would, he came lurking over to the barn, scanning the area to make sure that no one witnessed the sin that he would soon commit. That same scary, grim smile was spread across his face when he walked in. The small space quickly scented with his dirty, sweaty stench. It was a concentration of the odor that I'd smelt all week. My bowels churned and my heart tried to beat away from me. He stood there for what seemed forever just grinning, hands on his hips, and stripping me with his eyes. I didn't know who was supposed to speak first—not that I could. My throat had closed, making it too difficult to swallow, let alone speak. I can't do this. What the hell was I thinking?

"You just can't stay yo' fast tail outta trouble, can you?" He shook his head disapprovingly, but his wicked grin contradicted the false impression that he was trying to give. He took three heavy footsteps and was standing right over me like a big black cloud, blocking the little sunlight that there was. Déjà vu. Only this time, I knew what was coming. I wanted to haul ass out of there, but my legs wouldn't move. I felt like a ton of silly putty—useless and helpless. Tears welled, but this time I couldn't even try to contain them. They flooded my face and I felt like a damn fool having put myself in this position. Who I was fooling? I was just a girl, a big baby and a crybaby at that.

"Hush all that noise, gal! Who you thank you fooling? You must like it. Else you wouldn't be here."

He unbuckled his pants and the walls felt as if they were closing in on us. The rest of the world was shut out. Soon I would be muted and vandalized. He grabbed the back of my head and pushed my face in his midsection. I shook myself free. He grabbed at my legs, pulling them apart. I clawed into his fingers, piercing my nails into his skin until it broke. He snatched his hands back.

"What the hell wrong witchu?" he asked, looking down at his hands then reached for me again.

"Leave me alone less you plan on paying me," I blurted out.

Chapter 2

D eacon Russell was my first customer, paying just enough to
make my doings feel even more like a sin. I reasoned that it
was only a means to an end. A few years back, I'd overhead
my aunt talking about her trip down to New Orleans and all the
fun that she had. Life, as I knew it, got a little more tolerable from
that point on. I, then, knew that everything in Coushatta was
temporary.

I still didn't feel good about what I was doing and it still made
my skin crawl, but it only bothered me when I allowed my
thoughts to travel down that long, dark gutter of disgust and
depression. The more my coffer filled with dollars, the further that
gutter was growing out of reach and skin crawling was getting to
be not as bad.

My confidence was mounting too. I'd learned the effect that I
had on men and my existence was a fiend for it. Reverend Godsley
completed the lesson on my effect on men. All men: young and
old, rich and poor, married and single, Christian and heathen. They
would all go to any length to have what was between my legs.
Being that most of my customers were in the church, including a
Reverend—the terms, Christian and heathen, were becoming
synonymous.

Reverend Godsley is not to be confused with Rev. There was a
big difference. Rev was black. Reverend Godsley was white. Rev
preached on our side, but Reverend Godsley preached on the other
side of the tracks. Folks on the other side of the tracks had "old

money," as Mama would say, and they tithed their ten percent plus some.

Reverend Godsley had money and he ain't mind spending it on me. He didn't even want to put his thing in me. Hell, he didn't even really want me to touch him. He was obsessed with my behind and loved to use his hands and his mouth on it. Disgusting, I know. But hey, it floated his boat and built mine. We didn't get together as often as I would have liked. Otherwise, I would have been met my goal, plus.

After about a three month absence, I reckoned that he had repented and moved on. I dropped three other customers when I met him, so that meant that I had to go crawling back. That is, until I got another one from across the tracks that could afford my new prices. The prices set by Girly didn't sit right with me. It was money, yeah, but hell, it would have taken forever to reach my goal. I wasn't taxing for fun. I had a mission. I suggested that Girly up her prices too. She waved her hand dismissively.

"Girl, I been did that! You slow!"

Not knowing if she was telling the truth or lying, I left it alone. I'd come to learn that Girly was a shallow liar. She could lie quicker than I could part my lips to speak. I should've known since she had a gap. Mama warned to be mindful of folk with gaps because they lie. Either way, whether she had upped her prices or not, I was getting mine. My goal would be reached.

Girly changed the subject from prices to this cousin, Trouble Man, of hers. She had mentioned him a time or two before. He was coming home from war along with a buddy of his. Supposedly they would be loaded down with money; money that they couldn't spend overseas. I ain't buy too much into it.

Trouble Man had to have been the best story Girly ever told. Walter 'Trouble Man' Perkins. The mere thought of him made me bite my bottom lip. He was tall— towering a whole foot over me. His skin was black with a hint a purple: the shade of the ripest blackberry after the sun hit it at just the right angle. His dark brown eyes were adorned with lashes long and thick enough to make a woman jealous. His boyish smile tickled my guts. His body was chiseled by the Lord himself and had slavery still existed and he was standing on an auction block, he would have been rather expensive.

I dreamed about him when I was awake. I dreamed about him when I was sleep. I'd memorized his scent, his sound, and his smile. A cute, crooked smile. More like a smirk, just a curl at one corner of his mouth. Sexy. Deep, dark brown eyes complimented his dark chocolate skin. Ooh, I wanted his baby. All of us did. Our mamas could smell the heat rising from our panties and warned us about that one. That one would take you for all you're worth and leave you without a second thought. That one valued life as much as a penny lying in the parking lot. That one lied, cheated, and stole.

And boy did that lying, cheating thief have a hold on me! I could sense when he was near way before I saw him. And at night when I was in bed, under the covers, I played around inside of my panties, pretending that it was him. He was on my mind like freedom to a slave. Like whiskey to a drunk. Like sex to a virgin. Like water to the thirsty and food to the hungry. Oh, I could go on and on. In my mind, that one was my man.

But only in my mind.

See, men that fine liked the yellow type. Types like Bella Rose, Jessie Lee, Joyce Ann, and Priscilla with her pitiful self. They didn't like the brown skinned ones like me and Girly. Or at least that's what Girly said. She said that she'd overheard him say it and I believed her until the day that he claimed his brother's spot in my life. Me and Girly were downtown, as usual, smoking our cigarettes and talking shit. I couldn't tell you what we were talking about, but from the time that we passed the post office, I remember everything that was said like it happened five minutes ago.

He was somewhere in the vicinity, I could feel it. I could smell him. He had me wide open and didn't even know me. He walked out of the post office and stood at the bottom of the steps. He had both of his hands in his pockets and a toothpick in the side of his delectable lips. I wanted to kiss his top lip, his bottom lip, and each corner. I kept my eyes forward as we passed him. Girly arched her back, stuck her titties out, switched her hips, smiled, and waved like she was in some kind of pageant.

"Heyyy, Trouble Man."

He nodded in return and eyed me hard enough to count the hairs on my head. My heart skipped a beat then sped up to make up for the missed one. I focused on my shoes to make sure I didn't trip and fall on my face like I'd imagined myself doing so many times before. In the same breath, I wanted him to say something to me personally, then again I didn't. I wouldn't know what to say in return. I wasn't sure that I'd be able to look in his eyes and talk right at the same time.

"Say, girl. Ya ma ain't teach you to speak?"

He spoke to me. My man spoke to me. I had dreamed of that moment for months, but when it came time to speak I couldn't find my voice—just a big, stupid grin. My legs wobbled clumsily and my face flushed then flashed with heat as if all the blood from my legs rushed to my face. I shot my hand up like a Nazi and kept it moving. Thinking back, I must've looked like a damn fool.

"I think I deserve a more personal hello now. Come over here, girl. I won't bite."

He turned his lip up into that bad boy grin and either I was sweating something mean down there or he had me just that excited. The way he smiled while his eyes penetrated me said he knew it. Like he could smell it and he licked his lips like he could taste it.

My hands trembled so bad that I dropped my smoke and damn near burned my leg. Girly caught it like it was her last breath, smiled, and kept smoking. I wished that I could be cool, under all circumstances, like her.

"I almost thought you were one of those girls from New York the way you walked past me and didn't speak."

I blushed. Girly laughed.

"She ain't never been out of this rinky dinky town a day in her life. I've been up north a few times. You were in the Army, but I bet you ain't never been to North Carolina before," she teased.

"Nah. Don't care to. The South is the South. I like to sit next to a white man on the bus e'ry now and then," he chuckled.

"North Carolina is the North, boy," she nagged.

He ignored her. Well, we ignored her.

"Whatchu doing tonight?" he asked me.

"I don't have any plans," I answered, finally finding my voice. Then I wondered if I should've said that. Maybe I should've lied and said that I did have plans so my life wouldn't sound as stale as it really was.

"It's Friday night and you have no plans, ay? Well I gotta do something about that. Fine lil lady like yourself ain't got no business being in the house on a Friday night."

My mama would have a cow and a horse if I even *asked* if he could take me out. So I didn't. I just went. He was worth the ass whooping and the one after that and the one after that too. To me, he was worth her finding out about me losing my virginity and even getting put out over it. He was my man. Since I had a man, couldn't nobody tell me shit. I felt greater than girls my age and equal to those like my mother. I figured it wasn't nothing they had that I didn't either. We both had titties and a twat. Yeah, she had a house, but I would too, soon.

Problem was, soon wasn't coming soon enough. I had issues and the main one was Deacon Russell. From the time that I dropped him, he started being a creep. Me and Girly could be down by the bridge skipping rocks and he would show up. He went from glancing at me in church to full-on staring. The worst part of all was when he started coming around the house pretending to like my mama just so he could bother me. He would corner me in rooms and try to feel on me. I would slap his hands off and that pissed him off.

Girly thought it was funny. I did too until he walked in on me taking a bath one day. When he first came over, I went to my room to take a nap so that I wouldn't have to see him. Everybody was gone when I woke up—or, so I thought. I hopped in the tub so that I wouldn't have to argue with Etta, who spent hours on end in the bathroom, over who was going to go first.

When I could, I liked to fill the tub all the way the up, lay back, close my eyes, and pretend that I was someone very important, far away from Coushatta, and in my palace. That's exactly what I was doing when he walked in on me. I didn't even open my eyes; I just yelled that I was already in the bathroom. When I didn't hear a response or hear the door close back, I opened my eyes. He was standing over the tub with his shirt unbuttoned. He liked for me to rub all of that nappy chest hair of his before going down to touch his thing.

"Where's my mama?" I asked, trying to cover all my parts with my hands.

He smiled. "She had to make a run and told me to keep an eye on you."

"I don't need you watching me. Now get out of this bathroom so I can get dressed."

"I think I like you better just like that there," he said, reaching his hands down into his pants. He reminded me of an animal. It was like he couldn't help himself. His eyes would get real big, he

21

would start sweating and breathing heavy, and couldn't keep his hands to himself.

"If you put your nasty hands on me, I'ma tell," I warned.

"Well I reckon I better give you something worth telling."

And that's exactly what he did. He yanked me out of the tub and carried me to my room. I scratched, kicked, bit, and screamed, but I wasn't strong enough or loud enough. He threw me down on Etta's bed and took what he claimed to be his. He made me bleed as if it were my first time all over again. Even worse, he taught me how to hate.

I hated him and I hated my daddy, whoever the hell he was. I hated my mama and I especially hated Etta. She pranced around smiling, humming, and complaining about not having the right colored ribbons to match her outfits. Then, as if it really were all that mattered in the world, Mama would haul off and spend her last dime to find the damn ribbons.

Since it bothered me so much, I made it my business to throw the ribbons away. All of them. Every color and size. After realizing what I'd done, she busted through the bathroom door, accusing me of being a thief. Those were her first two mistakes right there. Number one: You don't walk in on me while I'm in the bathroom. Number two: Don't go pointing your finger in my face if you don't have proof. Number three: I hated her! So I grabbed a handful of her "headful of beautiful hair" that Mama would go on and on about and gave her the same kind of ass whooping that mama reached over her, so many times before, to give to me.

Mama was in the kitchen cooking and as usual, and when she heard all the commotion, she called my name. I let Etta go and stormed up to the front, ready to get the remaining shit off of my chest. Sure enough, we ended up going at it. I don't remember who said what first and who said what next, but I remember clear as day when she called herself throwing a bible verse at me. I caught it and threw it right back to her ass.

"Honor thy father and thy mother so that your days may be long. I know how it goes, but don't you think that the child should at least know who thy father is? Huh? Or does thy mother not know?"

A slap sounded off in the house and the left side of my face stung. My jaw pulsed with a rhythm to it. With each beat, I felt my jaw swell. I balled my fist, my nostrils flared. My face and neck got hot and if I was white, then I would've been red. Etta ran to the kitchen.

"Luke chapter 6 verse 29 says if someone strikes thy left cheek, turn to him your right cheek also." I turned my head and patted my right cheek signaling for her to strike it. "Ain't that what comes next, Mama? Answer me god dammit!"

She banged the countertop and raised her arm. I winced, but nothing happened. I peeked through one open eye to see what had saved me. Etta was holding Mama's arm in mid-air and in her trembling fist was a knife.

I backed out of the kitchen, down the porch steps, and hauled ass down the street. I had to get out of there. I didn't have anything to my name, but the clothes on my back. Girly's house wasn't far away, fortunately. I ran up the porch and banged on the door. The metal screen door rattled beneath my fist.

Eugene came to the door. I was shaking too bad to say anything. I just kept looking behind me like a woman in a horror movie. He looked around and opened the door. My heart slid back down into my chest. He draped his arm around my shoulders. The armpit of his white t-shirt looked like piss stains and smelled even worse, but I didn't care; they were havens right now.

"Don't w-w-worry," he responded to my thoughts. He smiled his sheepish grin again. His house smelled old, like mothballs. The stench clogged my throat like thick cod liver oil.

"W-w-what's wrong, Louisa?" he drawled. His long, dangly arms were outstretched. His big, pink lips spread into a grin. I shook my head, still unable to find my voice. Was my mama really going to kill me?

He led me to a dirty floral couch. The pillows sunk in. He helped me sit as if I was handicapped. I sat on the edge of the sofa, afraid of falling through. He went to the kitchen, grabbed a mason jar from a cabinet with the door hanging off the hinges, and rinsed it out in the sink. He filled it with tap water, no ice, and handed it to me. I sat it down on the coffee table, where I intended for it to stay for the remainder of the evening.

"W-w-what happened?" he asked, concerned. He sat on the green, corduroy chair on the other side of the room.

"Obviously I don't want to talk about it, Eugene," I snapped.

"W-w-well you w-w-welcome to stay here fo' a few days. M-m-my folks gone up to Georgia. G-g-girly gone too."

I looked around the room, roaches scattered up the pinewood walls. Some camouflaged in the dark spots on the walls. I shuddered before deciding that I'd rather sleep with the witch than with the roaches. Damn that.

"I was j-j-just 'bout to f-f-fry some poke chops." His thick unibrow rose.

I waved my hand. "I'm okay." My stomach growled, rebelling.

"You sho'll is pretty, Louisa. Even witcho' h-h-hair all over yo head like dat. C-c-can I touch it?" He got up and walked toward me.

Embarrassed, I grabbed at my hair. Then I realized that I hadn't put on a brassiere. I bent over, shielding my chest. He came over and sat beside me. A whiff of musk invaded my nose. He grabbed my hand.

Just as I was about to ask him for some space, the front door opened. The screen door slammed shut, rattling. My heart beat, I looked at Eugene for the okay.

"It's just my brother."

Trouble Man walked through the front door. He gazed down at me with the dreamiest set of eyes that I'd ever seen. His lips were full and had a tint to 'em from smoking cigarettes. I didn't mind though. I actually kind of liked it on him.

"Lil bro!" He walked over and nudged Eugene. He looked from Eugene, then me, and then back at Eugene. He stood there beaming with pride as if he'd won first place. Trouble Man licked his lips and smirked. I felt my panties moisten.

He slapped Eugene on the shoulder. "You didn't offer your lady a coke, a beer? Nothing?"

Eugene looked at the floor. "We don't have any."

Trouble Man shifted his body to one side, digging in his pockets. He pulled out a wad of money and handed Eugene two dollar bills. Trouble Man looked at me. "Coke or beer?"

I licked my lips and straightened my posture. I wanted him to see me as a woman. "Beer," I answered.

Eugene looked at me, confused. I ignored him.

"Go get us all a beer." He plopped down on the couch with his arms outstretched.

Eugene bent down and kissed me on my cheek. I couldn't possibly think of anything worse he could've done. Embarrassed and disgusted didn't half describe how I was feeling.

"I'll be right back, Louisa." I waited until the door shut behind him to wipe the kiss from my cheek.

Trouble Man got up to turn the TV on. He adjusted the antennas until the static cleared. A rerun from *I Love Lucy* was on. I slowly scooted back onto the sofa and got comfortable. That was my all-time favorite show. I knew every episode word for word. I downplayed my excitement, so as not to look like a child. After the show went off, an awkward silence took over.

"How old are you, Louisa?" he asked.

My heart upped its beat. "Seventeen," I lied. "But I'll be 18 next month," I added.

I noticed that I was scratching the insides of my palms and chewing on the inside of my jaw. I stopped. I tried to be cool and just watch TV.

"So you're just about a grown woman then, right?" He smirked. He had the kind of eyes that when he looked at you, it was like he was daring you to do something. He stood up and walked my way. My heart was beating a mile a minute. I swallowed, hoping my nerves went down. "You gon' make me sit in the hole?" He pointed at the sinking end of the couch.

I scooted over. He plopped down beside me. His weight caused me to sink a little further down. His scent was manly, but not stinking like his brother's. A mix of emotions and hormones swirled in the pit of my stomach. Suddenly, I no longer hungered for food. I craved trouble.

He pulled a pack of Marlboro cigarettes out of his front pocket and offered me one. I hesitated, and then grabbed one. He smirked. He put one in his mouth; he pulled out a white lighter. My mama's superstition came to mind: Burning things with white lighters is bad luck.

I took a long pull from the cigarette and choked. My eyes watered. He laughed out loud at me that time. He pulled from his cigarette, sat back and got comfortable, showing me that it was possible to be even more nervous than what I was already was. If I was going to make this work, then I needed to grow up. Since I didn't have it in me at the moment, I'd just have to pretend to be somebody else. I'd gotten pretty good at that. I took my time and took another pull from the cigarette. It tasted disgusting and dried my mouth out. I coughed again, but choked less that time.

"You from Coushatta?" he asked.

"Yeah."

"You like it here?"

I looked over at him. He was looking back at me, waiting on my response. He seemed genuinely interested. "No, I hate it actually."

"You plan on moving?"

"My mama said ain't nothing else past Coushatta but trouble." I frowned.

"How long you gon' let your mama tell you what to do?" he taunted, smirking.

I shrugged. I regretted saying that. Certainly, I must have sounded like a child. I looked out the window, wishing that Eugene would hurry up and come back.

"My brother gone for a while. The store is a good mile and half up the road." He laid a hand on my thigh.

My heart started racing again. I bit my lip. I pretended to be Girly, but that didn't work. Pretended that I was Josephine Baker and that was working okay until he leaned over and kissed my neck. "You like me, don't you?" He grinned. His breath against my neck made the room spin. I was to the point of just wanting him to undress me and get it over with it. This anticipation was killing me.

I bobbed my head up and down. He scooted closer to me and put my hand on his lap. His private was hard, very hard. It jumped. I snatched my hand back. He smiled. "I like you too. Ever since that day I saw you at the post office, I could only think of how pretty you were and…" he rubbed the side of my face, reminding me that it was swollen, "…and on top of that, you're a woman with her own mind. It don't get no better than that." He grabbed my breasts and I wished that I had on a brassiere. I swallowed.

He put my hand back on his lap. I rubbed it, feeling like that was the woman thing to do. He unzipped his pants, pulled out his private, and leaned back. I held it in my hand not really knowing what to do with it. He lifted my shirt and started sucking on my breasts. I whimpered. He looked up at me, smirked, and continued suckling. I rubbed my thighs together trying to rid the edginess in my pants. The seam of my pants rubbed against my boudoir which only made the feeling worse. He stopped sucking and reached for my zipper. I moved his hand.

He scrunched his face. "Whatchu doing? I thought you wanted this."

I swallowed. "I do, just not right now. Not here." I looked around the room. It went against every fantasy I'd ever had of him. If I fucked him there, he'd never think much of me. Plus, we'd have to rush because Eugene was coming back. I wanted to be where we would truly be all alone. Where he could lay me down and kiss me all over first. Where I could close my eyes and not have to worry about roaches getting in my hair.

He undid my pants anyway and slid his hand inside. "You a woman. Women do what they want…" He kissed my forehead. "When they want…" He kissed my lips. "And with who they want." He cupped my breast and kissed my nipple.

I exhaled slowly. He went back to undoing my pants. Suddenly, I felt comfortable. He rubbed his middle finger up and down my boudoir. I bit my lip to hold back a moan. Both of my nipples hardened. He slowly inserted his finger inside of me. Shocked, I jumped. It wasn't my first time or anything, but it was with the man of my dreams. He leaned in and kissed me. He parted my lips with his warm, sweet tongue.

Our tongues danced, for what seemed like hours. It felt like he owned my body; he knew just what to do to make me feel good. My body began to tremble. Embarrassed, I tried to pull away.

I exhaled slowly. He went back to undoing my pants. Suddenly, nothing else mattered. I felt as comfortable as I was gon' get. He rubbed his middle finger up and down my private. I bit my lip to hold back a moan. Both of my nipples hardened. He slowly inserted his finger inside of me. Shocked, I jumped. It wasn't my first time or anything, but it was with *him*. He leaned in and kissed me. He parted my lips with his warm, sweet tongue and I gave him mine in return. Our tongues danced for what seemed like hours. He owned my body, knowing just what to do to make me feel good. My legs started trembling. It wasn't because I was nervous. I just…I don't know. It never happened to me before. Embarrassed, I tried to pull away.

"It's okay. Let it go, baby." I felt myself contracting, and then I heard sloshing noises. I'd soused his hand. I was so embarrassed. He plunged his tongue into my mouth. Harder this time, and we kissed again. I heard the front door rattle and jumped to my feet. Eugene walked in, wiped the sweat from his brow, and smiled. He looked down at Trouble Man, smirking, and wiping my spit from his mouth. He dropped the bag of beer on the couch and just stood there looking at me. I stood up and brushed past him and dashed out of the house.

Chapter 3

T he only person tI could tolerate during that time was my
Trouble Man. Mama couldn't stand him. She called him a
reckless fool and called me everything, but what her beloved
Reverend would approve of. She would compare me to Etta,
reminding me that Etta was still in school; Etta had the brains and
better looks and was therefore, guaranteed to make something of
herself. Etta would eat that shit up too. She actually started
believing that she was better than me.

What she didn't have was Trouble Man. Did she want him?
Yes, it was all over her face and she couldn't wrap her tiny skull
around the fact that everything Mama hyped her up to be wasn't
enough to win him over. He wanted me and I never let myself
forget that. Even when I would catch his eyes roaming over other
women's bodies, I reminded myself that he wanted me. When I
caught him winking at other women, it didn't matter because if he
wanted them, he would've had them, but instead, he was with me.

When Girly claimed that she caught him screwing a white
woman across the tracks with her own two eyes, I called her a liar.
She described what they both had on, where they were, what time
it was, and even though I believed her deep down, I dismissed it
all as lies. She was just jealous and a jealous woman wasn't to be
trusted; or, at least that's how Mama would warn Etta about me.
Girly even had the nerve to say that Trouble Man raped her and
that's when I had to give her a piece of mind.

"You should be ashamed of yourself for lying the way you
do," I said.

"I ain't lying, Louisa. I swear."

"You are too and you know why? Because you jealous. You can't stand seeing me happy when you so miserable."

"What you talking about?" she asked, crying like a baby.

"What you think I'm talking about? I'm talking about your lies. That's all you know how to do is lie. Weren't you the one who told me that it happens to all women? Well, what's the problem now? If he really did it, then why you sitting up here crying? Why you ain't 'taxing' him? You know why? 'Cause you lying. That's why!"

That was the end of that. She never said that we weren't friends anymore and neither did I. That was the type of conversation that forever sealed things off without a declaration ever having to be made. My friendship with Girly was over and what hurt the most was finding out that at least half of things she accused him of was true. He was screwing a woman that lived across the tracks. One night he stood me up, but instead of going home and crying about it, I decided to check the spot that Girly had claimed to catch him at. The bridge.

A big white Cadillac was parked down under the bridge where folk like to fish at during the day. I didn't think much of it until I saw it move a little. I stopped and squinted my eyes so that I could see a little better and saw it shake again. I made my way down, being careful not to make any noise or be seen. I stooped behind a bush and continued watching the shakes and hearing the muffled moans that escaped from the car. Then, the car door opened and a blonde-haired woman stepped out. Her hair was a tangled mess, but she was smiling like she was having the time of her life. Who steps out next? Trouble Man.

My heart fell straight through me. It took everything in me not to run out from behind that bush and kill them both with my bare hands. I literally had to sit on them to keep myself still. Tears spilled down my face as if someone had died and when I saw the look on his face as he took her from behind, I died.

But I didn't leave. I stayed and watched. Words can't describe how disgusted I was at the fact that he was risking his life to do what he was doing. A lifetime in prison or a gunshot to the head wasn't nothing compared to do what would have happened to him had he gotten caught. Hadn't he heard what happened to that Emmett Till boy down in Mississippi? And all he did was whistle at a white woman.

I watched him stick his stuff back in his pants and kiss her goodbye before she climbed back into the driver's seat. Her headlights were so bright that I had to lay flat on my stomach to avoid being seen when she pulled off. By that time, I was ready to go, but I couldn't. Instead of walking off, he decided to sit on the edge of the river and have a smoke. He whistled some tunes while finishing off two cigarettes, at least. I could've come at that point. In fact, I should've. And, I would've too, had I been able to stop crying.

The most shameful part about that night was that I cried myself to sleep right there under the bridge. When I got home the next morning, Mama handed me a black bag full of every little thing that owned. She said that if I was woman enough to be laying up in sin all night, then I was woman enough to find somewhere to live. Etta stood behind her with her arms folded across her chest and her face twisted up like I was something stuck to the bottom of her shoe. I could've argued, but I didn't. I grabbed the bag, turned around, and left.

I went to Girly's house, where Trouble Man also lived. I was going to tell my friend that she was right and that I was sorry, but when I got there, she wasn't there; Trouble Man was. He was all smiles as if nothing had ever happened. The way he was acting had me wondering if it actually happened. Maybe I dreamt that it happened. But that couldn't be so. The black bag in my hand was foolproof that it actually happened because I actually fell asleep under the bridge and I actually got put out of my mama's house as a result.

Come to find out, Girly didn't even stay there anymore. She had moved out and had gone off to stay with some old man in Shreveport. Eugene didn't stay there either. He had joined the Army and was down in Texas somewhere at a camp. The house was far less cramped than I expected it to be and Trouble Man treated me like I was the only woman living. We were always together and that's the way I liked it.

Then, he got a job in Natchitoches which was a half hour away. Fortunately, I found an all-girl's school around the corner from his job. It was a domestic school which meant that we learned how to sew, cook, clean, and take care of babies. It was worse than traditional school and I gave the teacher a run for her money. While she only had to show the other girls how to do things once or twice, she had to walk me through everything step-by-step every time. I hated it, but at least it kept me busy and kept me close to my man. Plus, when the time came, it was sure to make me a better wife to him.

Marrying him was about the only thing that occupied my mind. That is, until he started staying out late. He would say that he was going to have a drink or two with a friend and would be home sooner than later. Then, sooner would become later...and later. I would fuss and he would promise to me that he was doing nothing wrong. So, I decided to loosen up a little. Then, his later got even later. He would come back home smelling like other women and even had the nerve to have a lipstick stain on his collar one night.

"Who were you messing around on me with?!" I screamed.

"What you talking about, woman?"

"I'm talking about the lipstick on your shirt," I answered him, poking at the stain.

"You put that there earlier," he said, kicking his shoes off.

"I ain't wore lipstick in months. You don't take me out anymore, remember?" I was trying my best not to raise my voice in his mama's house.

"Well I don't know how it got there then," he said, shrugging it off. "But I do know that it's late and I'm tired."

"I would be tired too if I was sleeping with every woman in town."

"That's enough, I said," he pointed at me.

"It was enough when I caught you messing with that white woman under the bridge," I mumbled under breath.

Out of nowhere and quicker than a snap of a finger, he had jacked me up on the wall. "What did you just say?" he asked through his teeth.

I was too scared to repeat it, so I lied. "Nothing."

"That's what I thought and I bet not ever hear you telling them lies again." With that, he dropped me. I was so far from the floor that instead of landing on my feet, I fell on butt. He didn't bother helping me up either. He stood there giving me the eye before turning and walking away.

I made my bed on the couch with the hole in it that night. The next morning, before he woke up, I was gone with no plans of returning. Since I didn't have anywhere else to go, I went to Rev's house. When his wife opened the door, she looked surprised and asked me why I hadn't been to church. I told her that my mama had put me out on account of what she thought she knew. So, they took me in for a couple of days. That following Sunday, they had bought me a brand new outfit for church: the dress, stockings, and patent leather shoes. The whole nine. When it came time to leave, they didn't take me back home with them though. Rev had a little talk with my mama. Whatever he said to her ended in her telling me to "come on."

I made it my business to be a little nicer. Although my mama had taken me back in, she still wasn't treating me any better. On top of that, I had no Girly or Trouble Man to turn to. So, I made an honest effort to befriend Etta again. After all, she was my sister. I made up in my mind that I didn't need anyone else. Me and Etta had been brought into this world together and we would leave together. I didn't need Mama, Girly, and especially not Trouble Man.

I had to tell myself stuff like that every day. I spent so much time trying not to think about him that I didn't even realize that focusing on not thinking about him was the same thing as thinking about him. Regardless of whether or not he was on my mind, under no circumstances would he ever touch me or talk to me again. I was through.

Not long after, a sharp rapping at the window woke me up in the dead of the night. Me and Etta jumped up at the same time. We looked at one another with mirrored expressions. After about four circles of you look, no, you look, I mustered the nerve to peek out of the curtains. It was Trouble Man. The sight of him made my heart skip a beat and my stomach flip. I missed him beyond belief, but the pain was still there. I had nothing because of him. No school, no Girly, and barely had a roof over my head.

But, I still loved him.

I still missed him and hated myself for it. It made no sense. Was that love? If so, then I was a fool to ever have wanted it in the first place. That wasn't the kind of love that I dreamt of. What I was feeling was more like sickness. I had no control of catching it and couldn't get rid of it to save my life. Thoughts would crawl into my bones and start eating away. Some days were better than others, but it just had to run its course, I guess. That felt like forever since the memories never stopped coming. Everything reminded me of that boy.

"What the hell you want? Didn't I tell you not to come round me no mo'?"

He looked around, nervously.

"You bet not be stirring no trouble round here. I live with my mama again case you forgot."

"I had to see you."

I looked over at Etta, who I had, for a second, forgotten was even in the room. She was looking at me, wide-eyed and unashamed, waiting to see what I would do next.

"Well I don't wanna see you." I pouted.

Dammit that sounded weak. My heart was like a battered woman trying to hide the bruises and the pain, trying to defend its last piece of pride, but it was beginning to tell on itself. I shouldn't have let the conversation go that far. I should have slammed the window shut in his damn face. But I didn't. Now it was obvious that I missed him and that I loved him and would forgive him and go back. I knew it, he knew it, and now Etta knew it too.

He beckoned for me to come out.

"Come on, shit," he spat.

His nerve! He messed this up. Not me. Messed up my whole life and sent me crawling back to my mama's house. Then after he realized that he messed up, he came crawling back and got the damn nerve to be irritated with me. As much as I wanted to spit in his damn face and tell him to go to hell, I liked it. I loved his edge; his audacity was like none other. The little heartbeat between my legs pumped a little harder. Dammit. I looked over at Etta who had screwed up her lip and her face, without words, asked me if I was serious. My expression softened and pleaded with her to understand, not to judge me, but most importantly…not to tell Mama!

She shook her head, disgustingly, and laid back down facing the wall. She couldn't understand and she refused to even try, but she wasn't going to tell our mama and that was the most important favor at the moment. I knew all of this without any words spoken. That was one of the perks of being twins, I guess. I climbed out of the window and grounded my feet.

He drew in a deep breath as one would before reciting an Easter speech.

"I missed you."

I rolled my eyes and sighed. I crossed my arms over my chest and looked everywhere around him. Anywhere, but in his eyes. He still made me nervous.

"Look here." He grabbed my arms, shaking me gently with each word. "Now I know I fucked up, but I ain't ready to let you go."

That made me laugh. This was one bold nigga here.

"What's funny?"

"What's funny?" I leaned forward as if straining to hear him better. "What's funny is that you can ruin my life like you did: kick me out, and then up and decide that you ain't ready to let go." I stepped forward, closer to him, feeling as tall as him, and just as bold. I was five hundred degrees and I was finally about to let him feel the heat. "You let go a long time ago. You let go when you stuck yo' thang in that white woman cross the tracks!" I yelled, pointing toward the railroad tracks.

He sighed. "How many times I gotta tell you? I ain't mess with that woman."

Still lying.

He took a step forward, meeting my stance and suddenly I began to shrink back down to my size.

"On my grandmama grave, I ain't mess with that woman."

"Stop putting yo' lies on that dead woman's grave."

I wanted to tell him that I had seen him with my own two eyes. That Girly only pointed me in the right direction, but I had witnessed it on my own. I seen the look in his eyes while he did it with that woman. It wasn't nothing like the look he gave me. He did her and enjoyed it. As much as I hated to admit it, that's the part that hurt the most. I would never tell him that though.

He pulled me into his chest and held me. I tried to fight him off, but to no avail. He gripped me tighter and my feelings resuscitated. I couldn't let him know. I couldn't keep chasing his whistles. I let my arms dangle at my sides. He buried his face in my untamed hair and inhaled. My heart began to beat wildly. I felt like the earth was turning into quicksand under my feet. I was losing my ground. My defenses were weakening. I had only a fracture of hope in the possibility of him changing, but every time he came around, that fracture was becoming whole again. I buried my face in his chest, closed my eyes, and inhaled deeply, filling my senses with him. And just like that, I had forgiven him.

"I love you, girl."

"I love you, too," I muffled in his chest. There I said it.

"Marry me, Louisa."

My heart dropped. My ears went deaf and my eyes went blind. My defenses were laddering their way back up, shutting down my senses. Marry him? How could I marry him and where was all this coming from? I had been the one raving on about marriage; he was always on the opposite end of the stick. I pulled while he pushed. What changed? Was it possible that my leaving taught him a lesson? Had he finally learned my value and grown afraid of losing me to the next man? Why was I stalling? I had waited so long to hear those words and there they were, but that wasn't how it was supposed to be said. He didn't even ask me, he told me. And wasn't the man supposed to get on one knee in front of my parents on a Sunday after church?

Oh hell, what in my life, ever turned out as I expected it to? Nothing. Obviously, I had life misunderstood. The way that I assumed that things should be done or should be said wasn't always so, including my proposal. I wasn't about to be no fool again though. He was my man and Lord knows I loved him. All six feet of him, his truths, his lies, his love, his hate. I loved it all. And if loving him was an illness, then dammit, I was just sick. Both of us. And if that meant that marrying him was a terminal illness then until death did us part, I was all in.

"Okay."

"Good. Let's go."

I laughed. "Let's go where, stupid? It's the middle of the night."

Again, he breathed heavily, looking around. "Anywhere, shit. Wherever you wanna go."

And that's how it happened. My dream had come true. I had finally made it to New Orleans. It wasn't the way I expected to make it there, but I'd already learned that lesson. Everything wouldn't go as I planned or wanted. New Orleans is what I had saved for, for so long. It's what I had traded in my dignity, my last string of innocence, and put up with so much for so long for. No one else had made it out of Coushatta. It had a way of sucking everybody right back in. It wasn't no going back for me though. That was my deal to myself. Whatever happens: Do. Not. Go. Back.

I couldn't do nothing for the first couple days in the city. My stomach was sour. It was as if my intestines had twisted themselves into a question mark, questioning if I lost my damned mind. After two days in a hotel room, one of Trouble Man's war buddies came through. He loaned us his late mother's house. It was small, smaller than my mama's house even, but perfect. It was fully furnished with pictures on the walls, a full fridge, and even smelled of a home.

Just not mine.

I felt like an intruder. Like at any moment, the real owners would show up. I could never relax. I only sat on the edge of the sofa. I swept the floors at least five times a day, washed every dish after every use, and even picked stray hairs from the pillows every morning. All in all, at least one of my concerns was gone; I had an address.

My other concerns still existed though. They still whispered in my ear while I slept at night. Like what kind of mother I would be, what kind of father Trouble Man would be, when he would start acting like a baby was on the way, and where I would go if this arrangement didn't work out.

It pained my mama to see me go. She would never admit it and hated for it to show, but it was all over her face. For her to be a woman of so many words, she had none. She said nothing. She didn't call me stupid, didn't tell me to think it over, didn't tell me that I shouldn't run off with a man who wasn't my husband, but what hurt me most was that she didn't try to stop me. Her lips were pursed, nostrils flared, and with her trembling hands she slammed the door in my face. Etta watched from our living room window. The look on her face said that she wasn't disgusted in me no more, she couldn't and wouldn't understand, but she pitied me. She pitied the fool.

Just as jobs seemed to come and go with Trouble Man, so did our addresses. As a matter of fact, I can't remember the entirety of any address that we shared together. We had become gypsies of the city. We always had enough to cover the down payment of one place, then a handful of excuses to get us by the next few months, and by the time of eviction, we were already moving into another place. It got so bad that we started having to use a third party—some innocent soul to set the apartment up for us. If there were some wanted list amongst the landlords, I'm quite sure that Trouble Man and I was number one.

My favorite of all our addresses was on South Claiborne Street. I can't recall the number of it, because like I said, we moved too much. It was a small, white double shotgun house. Two houses right next to each other, sharing the middle wall. I had to ask why it was called a double shotgun house. Our landlord explained.

"Well, if ya' stand dead in front da house wit' a double barrel shotgun..." he gripped his imaginary gun and squinted one eye, "...and shoot," he lowered his gun. "A bullet would fly tru' da front do' right tru' da back do'."

As the church folk back home would say, I rebuked that in the name of Jesus. It wasn't going to be no shooting around there. The only thing flying through doors would be love and good luck. To be sure, I stopped calling my new husband "Trouble Man" after we married down at the courthouse. I preferred to call him by his name, a man's name: Walter.

And he was being just that to me, a man. He'd gotten a good job working with a construction company downtown. They built nearly all the important buildings in the city: the new courthouse, Union Station, and the new City Hall. Not only was he able to pay all the bills, but we were able to start eating out again, buying things for our baby that was on the way, and I even had money left over to spend on myself. Things were looking up.

I made sure to mention it all in a colorful letter back home.

Chapter 4

O ur house on Claiborne was a twirl and a good tune away from the French Quarter. Good music, food, and people. Good days. On any given day, I would wake up to melodic brass right outside the front door. Parades for days and parties to last me the rest of my life. Walter worked more than twelve hours every day and I was spending money nearly just as fast. After all, there was nothing else for me to do.

Up until I had the baby, that is. Then, my whole world changed its direction and revolved around her. Walter fell in love with her from the time that she slid out of me covered in slime. I passed out right after that, and when I woke up, Walter had named her and was staring down at her in his arms like she was the best thing since sliced bread.

"What's her middle name?" I asked him.

"She don't need one. Her first name is just fine. Doris."

He never looked up at me once while talking to me. He never said thank you, I love you, or nothing. He just sat there with his finger inside of her closed fist, kissing her forehead every so often. I'd be a liar if I said that it didn't make me just a little jealous.

Had I known that all of that daddy-daughter time was going to end in the hospital, then I would've swallowed that jealously back down and let him keep her. It wasn't that he loved her any less after we left the hospital. It was just that his definition of loving was providing. Nothing more and nothing less.

That left me having to do everything by myself. I was either changing Doris' pamper, feeding her, burping her, bathing her, or putting her to sleep so that I could get dinner started and the house cleaned. Just when I'd lay down to close my eyes, Walter would come home with his breath smelling like he'd been at a bar all day instead of work. That wouldn't have bothered me so much had he just let me sleep, but no, he wanted to go sticking his thing up in me.

Had I had just an ounce of sense, then I would've stopped him. But I didn't. I feared that if I didn't let him handle his business, then he would do so with another woman. Then, before I knew it, I was a mother of not one, but three little girls: Doris and a set of twins, Mona and Reta. Wasn't nothing cute about it no more. Fortunately for me, I still maintained my shape. I didn't lose my waist line, get stretch marks, or need a girdle like most women who'd become wives and mothers.

Buildings were sprouting all over New Orleans and as the city grew I felt like I was growing with it. Like a native, I too, could recall the buildings before and after. I'd witnessed union stations being replaced, the old courthouse become new, the New Basin Canal become the Pontchartrain Expressway, and the Civil Rights Act come into play.

While they fought for the rights of all, I was busy fighting for my own rights. Walter was spending more money and time at the damn liquor store than he was at work. When I asked for money, I had to explain what I planned to buy with it and why I needed it. Then it got to be so bad that he just straight up stopped giving me money and dared me to ask for it. So when I would be out and about and black folk would ask me if I was joining them to march, protest, or sit-in, I would go off on 'em every time. Why in the hell should I care about trying to drink out of white folk's water fountain when the water in my own house was barely running?

I wanted to live under my own roof without having to steal from my husband's wallet to pay the rent only to get my ass kicked for it after he realized it. I was tired of being taken without permission, having to clean up his bodily fluids behind his drunk ass, and raise the girls by myself. If I was going to have to raise the girls alone, then let it be that. Let me go. He never would though. He threatened to hurt my babies if I ever left, knowing that I had nowhere else to go. I couldn't take the chance. Over time, he'd grown a look in his eyes that said that he no longer had a heart; he was capable of anything.

So I stayed. My life consisted of cleaning, cooking, and taking care of the kids, which was no easy task. Doris, for one, was a talkative ass child. She had every question in the world and refused to let anyone ignore her. She had the key to her daddy's heart and knew it. She was the only reason that he gave up a few dollars for me to make groceries. Reta and Mona, on the other hand, the twins, were some fussy ass babies. I never saw nothing like them. If they weren't sleep, then they were crying.

Doris would scream my name, which ended up waking them up and they would go to hollering. After a while, I would manage to get them back to sleep. Then one would wake up crying, only to wake up the other, and all hell would break loose again. The damn girls hollered until their voices went hoarse and then cried some more. Instead of sitting them down on somebody's porch and walking off like I had a good mind to do, I'd learned to mix a little whiskey into their milk. It didn't hurt them none; it just made them sleep longer and gave me a little peace of mind, is all.

When I said "a little peace of mind," that's exactly what I meant. It's hard to relax when you can't call a place home for more than two or three months. Add three kids, all under the age of three, on top of that and you'll get a glimpse of what I was going through. The best thing about the new address was that I finally found a friend, a white girl name Jewel.

We got along real good. She would watch the kids for me whenever I needed to go down to the market or whatnot and they loved her. As much as them hollering ass twins got on my nerves, they were nothing but smiles and giggles for Jewel. She would even sit down with motor-mouth Doris, drink apple juice in wine glasses with her, and have long conversations about only God knows what.

I guess I should've thanked her for that since neither me or her daddy was trying to hear what she had to say. I was too busy trying to worry about how we were going to survive after Walter lost his new job. It was sure to happen. He had fallen out of love with me, the kids, and the liquor, and substituted us with these tubes of powder that he would bring home. He called it his medicine.

At first, I didn't mind. He would be in a daze and lost in his own little world. Sometimes I would take advantage and leave him with the kids so that I could finally get a taste of the town with Jewel. That went on for a few months and I began relaxing again and trusting that life had gotten better.

Then he got another job, doing the same type of work, only to lose that one too. Once he stopped being able to afford his medicine, he lost his damn mind. He started off putting his hands on me when he found out that I stole his money. Then, he went to doing it when I turned him down for sex. Then, the hitting got worse, almost every day it seemed. He started beating me like I was a man and that's when I stopped fighting back. When he slung Doris, his beloved baby girl, across the room one evening, I should've taken it as my sign to leave. But like a faithful dog to his master, I stayed. As the old folks would say, every dog has its day though. Believe you, me.

That day came on August 2, 1961. I woke up on the kitchen floor, choking. I rolled over onto my side and spat out a mouthful of blood, and then realized the entire tile floor around me was covered in red. I stood up and the room started spinning, so I grabbed the kitchen counter to balance myself.

My panties were ripped and lying on top of the toaster. A mound of my own hair was matted on the floor beside my barefoot. I closed my eyes and tried to recall what had happened, but only could see orange spots. I limped to the bathroom, noticing that the walls were smeared. The air smelled musky and heavy. The twins were shut up in the room, hollering up a storm. *We must've been fighting again*, I thought.

I could barely recognize the woman who reflected back to me in the mirror. My eyes were swollen shut. My lips were puffed and broken. I coughed up blood that was so thick it looked black. I rinsed out the sink and splashed my face. I smiled to see if all of my teeth were still in place. They were. Satisfied, I turned the light off, limped to the kitchen, grabbed a cast iron pot, and limped to the living room. I was prepared for a round two, if necessary.

Walter sat in his chair—the raggedy green reclining chair—with his head leaned back. A pint of Taaka Vodka sat at his feet, still wrapped in the brown paper bag. His mouth was gaped open and his chest wasn't moving. *Had God finally answered my prayers and killed the bastard?* In a couple years, he had aged a decade. Dark rings circled around his drooping eyes, wrinkles sagged around his bone dry lips, and scabs and open sores speckled his limbs.

A rubber band was tied to a death grip around his arm and a rusted needle hung half way out. I removed it. He started coughing. His brown eyes rolled forward while his mouth still hung open. I raised the pot, just in case, so I'd be ready. He grabbed my leg and I swung, causing my shoulder to pop out of place. He groaned and I swung again. He fell face first on the floor and started shaking. I stood over him and hit him again. His body went limp and his wounds flooded the floor. Another blood bath.

I dropped the pot and limped back to the bathroom. I couldn't even tell you if the kids were still crying. My mind wasn't there. I walked straight past the mirror to the bathtub. I turned the rusted, screeching knob that was engraved with an H. I didn't even bother unbuttoning my dress; I just tore it off my body. My hair that was once long, thick, and full of life looked as dead as I felt. Flat and tangled.

A box of Epson salt sat on the sill next to the tub. I emptied the entire box into the tub and eased in the water which quickly turned pink, and then red. I scrubbed myself clean and lay back, resting my head on the edge of the tub. I felt myself drifting off to sleep and dreamt that I was cradling a baby, rocking in a rocking chair in a long, empty hall.

I heard Walter's heavy footsteps and woke up. It wasn't Walter, but the front door. I waited for him to open the door, but he didn't. Then it dawned on me. *I killed my husband.* The knocking on the door continued. I pulled up the drain and stepped out of the cold water. My headache was gone as well as my limp, but I still had to walk slowly. I threw on an old nightgown and walked to the front door. Jewel walked in, eyes wide open, and her quivering hands covered her mouth.

"Oh my God! What the hell happened here?" she asked.

"What it look like?" I stepped over Walter's body and plopped down on the sofa.

"Get some bleach water," she ordered.

I threw my head back and sighed. It wasn't even twelve o'clock yet and I felt like I had picked an acre of cotton, been whipped, and ran the underground railroad twice. I looked down at the red puddle on the floor. *I really killed him.*

"Louisa get up and get moving 'less you plan on spending the rest of your days in Orleans prison and trust me, it isn't nice. Especially the colored side."

I didn't budge.

She shook her head and cursed under her breath. Her heels pounded the floors all the way to the kitchen. I mustered up enough energy to follow her. She filled the bucket with bleach and water and grabbed sponges and towels. She got on her hands and knees, pulled up her sleeves, and started scrubbing the blood from the floor.

"Go get the kids," she said.

"They're alright," I answered.

"Fine," she said, standing to her feet. She handed me the sponge. "You clean and I'll go get the kids."

I got down on my hands and knees and picked up where she'd left off. Dirt, blood, and water foamed and splashed against the baseboards. It was a mindless task which was exactly what I needed at the moment.

She walked back in doing a side to side bounce, juggling the twins on her hips. Doris saw me and ran for the kitchen, but Jewel yanked her back. "I'm about to go feed them. We'll be back in a few," Jewel said. She stooped down so Doris could get on her back. She looked like a damn fool with three black babies hanging from her. On the way out, I heard her tell Doris to close her eyes and count to ten. I went back to scrubbing.

Before I knew it, she was back. She'd fed, cleaned, and put the kids down for a nap at her house. She walked right in, damn near giving me a heart attack. I saw that it was her, sighed in relief, and then went back to cleaning. I went over the floor a second time with fresh water and then a third time with some of my good rose water.

"I knew that it would end up like this. It was either you or him," she said. "That last time you came over with your face busted open, he cried for you to come back. Claimed that he would kill himself without you, would never hit you again, and you went crawling back." She chuckled.

"Spare me the judgment."

"It's not my place to judge you. That's not what I'm doing," she said. "It never made any sense to me." She stared unseeingly at the floor. "Walking around your own house on eggshells. Afraid to say the wrong thing, cook the wrong thing, walk the wrong way, breath the wrong way," she said.

"You say it like you lived it."

"Why you think I left Florida?"

She pushed her sleeves up, grabbed a sponge from the sink and joined me on the floor.

I shrugged. "You never told me, so I never asked. You killed him or something?"

"No, I didn't kill him." She dipped the sponge into the water and plopped the wet poof on the floor causing a splash. "I defended myself. He just so happened to die in the process."

I cracked a smile; my sore jaw bone popped out of place. Then, I noticed she wasn't smiling. She was dead serious. Right then, I appreciated her history. It was comforting in an odd kind of way. Misery really does love company.

"Louisa, I swear you just as country and naïve as you were when I first met you." She shook her head. She stood up, holding onto the counter top for support. "Where does he keep his smack?" she asked.

"His what?"

"His smack, his junk, his dope. Whatever you wanna call it. And the needle too."

"His medicine?"

She laughed. "Medicine. Now that's a good one. Louisa, please don't tell me he told you it was medicine and you believed him."

I didn't respond.

"Lord help her." She raised her arms and dropped them, helplessly. "Just go get it."

I slowly walked back to our bedroom, gliding my hands down the streaked walls for balance. I opened the top drawer of the dresser and unfolded his black church socks. The only damn purpose of them was to hold his medicine because he damn sure never stepped foot in church. I grabbed the bag of brown powder, closed the drawer, and walked to the living room.

She held out her hand. I put the bag in it.

"Where's the needle?" She asked.

I pointed under the sofa. She reached down and picked up the syringe with its rusted needle and put it on the table. She dumped some of the brown powder on the spoon. She pulled a white lighter from her brassiere and lit the bottom of the spoon.

She knew the procedure to the tee. I don't even think Walter whipped up his concoction faster than that. I started to ask her how she knew it so well, but decided against it.

"I see you. You want to ask me how I know how to cook junk. Don't you?" She asked.

I shook my head. "No. I was just gon' say that its bad luck to use a white lighter."

"Your face looks like road kill, you have a dead man at your feet, and you're worried about luck?"

I shrugged, wishing that I had just gone along with asking her how she knew how to "cook junk." The brown powder on the spoon started to bubble. She sucked the brown liquid through the syringe, flicked it twice and stabbed it in his arm. No hesitation.

I flinched. She chuckled.

"What's so funny?" I asked, annoyed.

"You."

"Me?"

"Yes, you." She handed me my cast iron pot. "Go put this back in the kitchen."

I took the pot from her.

"It's over?" I asked.

She whipped out another cigarette. "Almost."

"What else?"

"Well first off…" she paused to light her cigarette, "…don't tell anyone." She leaned in close to my face. "Don't even tell your damn self," she said, blowing smoke in my face.

"I know that," I said.

"Good. Next is to call the cops."

"Call the cops? Why? For what?"

"Who else is gonna get him out of here?"

"He can rot right here for all I care. The cops will lock my black ass up and toss the damn keys."

She's white. I'm black. The difference may be obvious, but Jewel didn't see things that way. Since the day she met me, color never mattered. She never acted like it was a difference. Today she'd see. A white woman can kill a man, drop some tears, and get a teddy bear and a bus ticket. Me on the other hand…

She placed both of her hands on my shoulders and looked me square in the eyes.

"Louisa," she said as if she were talking to Doris. "Why would you go to jail, sweetie? We came in from some shopping and found him like this. We don't know what happened. Maybe he overdosed."

She turned and left. I rushed to the kitchen to the pot away and followed her back to her house. I sat down on the plush, floral printed sofa. A copy of The Times Picayune sat on the coffee table. I picked it up and turned to the entertainment section. Josephine Baker, my idol, was coming to New Orleans—her second favorite place in the world, next to Paris: Josephine Baker Performs at Club 500 Friday, March 13, 1959.

"Ready?" She asked, walking in wearing a new dress.

"No."

"Let's get this over with." She walked off. I got up and followed behind her.

"And just what am I supposed to say?"

"Well what happened?"

I took a deep breath. "We came in from shopping and I found him dead on the floor. I think he overdosed."

"Good." She handed me the phone receiver. "And say it like you mean it." She spun the rotary dial three times and folded her arms over her chest.

"9-1-1," the operator answered.

My heart started racing and my hands shook just as fast. "I JUST CAME HOME AND FOUND MY HUSBAND DEAD!" I screamed. Jewel smiled and gave me the thumbs up.

I gave the operator my address and she assured me that help was on the way. I handed Jewel the phone and she hung it up.

"That wasn't so bad was it? Now the cops will be here in less than 5 minutes." She looked me up and down. "You were out shopping in that?"

I looked down at my thin, frilly nightgown. I went back home and ran straight through the living room, afraid to look at Walter, and into the bedroom. I grabbed the first dress I saw and threw it on. I slipped on my flats and ran back next door. Soon as I got back in the house good, the sirens pulled up. Jewel walked up front, cool as ever.

"IT'S THE POLICE. OPEN UP!!" A deep voice on the other side of the door yelled. Through the window, I could see a figure trying to peek in the blinds. "MA'AM IF YOU CAN HEAR ME, WE'RE HERE TO HELP. OPEN UP!"

I looked at Jewel. She looked back at me, annoyed, pointing at the door, beckoning for me to open it. I opened the door to two officers. Both white men in black uniforms with black peaked caps. One of them looked to be my age. The other one was old enough to be my daddy.

"Did you call for police?" the older officer asked.

I bobbed my head up and down. "Yes, sir"

"Is your husband in here?" he asked, looking around behind me.

"No, sir. I live next door."

"Then why the hell are we standing here? Show me the crime scene."

The older officer walked in and looked around. The younger officer fingered the gun on his hip, still standing in the doorway.

"What we got Searg?" the younger officer asked.

The officer held up one finger, silencing him. He looked at me, then over at Jewel, back at me, then back at Jewel. He walked over to Jewel, put a hand on her shoulder and asked her was she okay. She bobbed her head up and down and he draped his arm across her shoulder. He looked back at me with squinted eyes, and then walked with Jewel to the kitchen. She broke out into a sob.

I crossed my fingers behind my back, hoping that she wouldn't tell. The other officer walked over to me with his hands still on his gun. He asked me what happened. I told him. Walter had beaten me to a pulp, so I left. I came back and found him dead. He looked over my shoulder at the body, still not moving, and nodded his head.

Jewel and the sergeant walked back up front. Jewel was calmer, her face relieved. She held onto her rosary. I feared that she'd either "confessed our sin" or pulled it off. I prayed the latter. The sergeant went over to Walter, stood over him, and patted the side of his face twice. He picked up his wrist, checking for a pulse, and then dropped it. The deadweight hit the floor.

"Dead as a deer behind my rifle," he said, stepping over the body. "You got plans for a funeral?" he asked.

I hadn't even thought about that. At the same time, I knew that I couldn't afford a funeral. I shook my head no.

"Can't blame you. Damn junkies don't deserve a funeral anyhow," he said, clicking his tongue. "Say, yung'n, grab the black bag out the trunk."

The rookie officer nodded his head and ran out to the car. He came back with a big black bag. The sergeant unzipped the bag and they stooped down at Walter's sides. They counted to three and lifted, grunting.

"He's a big'un."

They dropped him in, zipped the bag back up, and carried him outside to the car. I felt my blood boiling. They tossed him in the backseat like trash. I clinched my jaw.

Chapter 5

B *oom. Ba. Boom. Boom. Boom. Boom.* I jumped, and then realized that it was only the door. My nerves were a mess.

After Walter died, I started having crazy dreams. The only thing in common with each dream was a crazy looking black woman. I didn't know who she was or what she wanted from me. I would wake up hollering at the top of my lungs, but could never remember them enough to tell anybody else about them.

I peeked out of the curtains and saw a white Fiat at the curb. It was Mr. Russeau. Before I could open the door, he was tapping on the window on the side of the house. *Just what the hell does this sap sucker want this early in the morning?* I pressed my back against the door, praying that he wouldn't wake the kids. I stayed there until I was sure that he was gone, then tiptoed back to the kitchen.

I had forgotten about my food on the stove. My egg had fried black and the grits were scorched and popped like mines in a warzone, daring me to come close. As I poured cold water over the pots, I liked'ta cried. When it rains on me, it doesn't just pour. The whole damn roof caves in.

The eerie feeling of being watched called me to turn around to Mr. Rousseau, standing at the kitchen doorway, rocking on his heels and swinging those damn keys.

"Who gave you permission to come in my damn house?" I screamed. I charged toward him like a bull that had found its red target. Reality sunk in. I stopped and folded my arms across my heaving chest. His smirk cracked into a clown smile. I wanted to hammer my fists into his fat freckled face.

"Technically, my name is on this house, making it mine. Not to mention that it's the first of the month. Rent is due by nine a.m. and it is now…" flicking the face of his watch forward, he added, "…ten minutes 'til ten."

"Walter passed a few days ago, leaving me and the kids to fend for ourselves. Now if you give me a few days, then I'll have your money for you."

"Whoa! Stop right there!" He roared laughing and raised a hand as if his kidneys couldn't withstand not another joke. Only I wasn't joking. He readjusted his belt up over his rotund mound of a belly, regaining his composure. He wiped a tear from the corner of his eye. "Miss Perkins, I have a waiting list long as the Mississippi for this here space. Some offering to pay double. Why, in my right mind, wouldn't I take this chance to collect those extra pennies?"

Mama always said to wear some pride on your right shoulder. Don't go around weeping and whining about your problems. Folks don't wanna hear about it and if they do, then you had best be wary of their heart's intentions. She also said that folks are liable to cast out their upbringing when backed against a wall. Well, I was backed against that wall and didn't have a pot to piss in, or a window to throw it out of.

"If you could give me about a week, I can have that money for you. All I need is a week."

"No can do. On the first of every month, including New Year's Day, I go around to collect what's mine. Now whether that's rent or my property is up to you."

"I ain't got nowhere to go. I don't even know nobody. You can't do this to me. Not right now."

"Oh, but I can. And will too. Unless of course…" he looked up at the ceiling with a smirk on his face, then begun his heel-to-toeing again, waiting on me to fill in the blank.

I didn't see my first homeless person until I set foot in New Orleans. Coushatta didn't allow people to go homeless. We looked out for one another. Talked plenty shit about each other, but would never let another fall that far down.

I had two choices and they were both tapping their foot and checking the time. I could either sleep with Satan Clause for a roof over my head or sleep with Mother Nature with the bridge over my head. What did I do? What I had to do, that's what.

He pinched my nipples and instructed me to go to the bedroom, undress completely, and to leave my panties on the doorknob. I reminded myself that I was doing what I had to do, what any woman would do, including my mama.

I unbuttoned my house coat, along with pride, folded it neatly, and sat it at the foot of the bed. I slid down my panties and realized that the pangs in my stomach weren't just from hunger. A smile spread across my face. *He may not come when you want Him, but He'll be there right on time.*

Two sharp knocks at the door interrupted my humming session. The door opened. Mr. Rousseau stood there, wearing as much as he did when he popped out of his mama's snatch. Unashamed, too, as if he was the first thing smoking on my Christmas list.

"What happened to the panties being on the doorknob? You're ruining a perfect fantasy. Unless of course…" he chuckled a low I-know-what-you're-up-to type of laugh, "…you were expecting me and happened not to be wearing any."

He looked me up and down, grinning like I was a steaming gourmet three course meal. I shoved the panties at him so fast, you would've thought we were playing hot potato.

"I'm on the rag."

"Is that right?"

"If I'm lying, I'm flying. The proof is in your hand, there." I grabbed my house coat.

"Is that right?"

"Come back five days from now and we'll finish what we started," I lied.

In my mind, God had just granted me five days to come up with his money and I intended to do just that. Mr. Rousseau had something else in mind though. He flopped down on the bed and every mound of fat flopped right along with him. He lay back with one hand resting behind his head. A big stupid grin spread across his face and he rubbed his inflated stomach with his other hand.

"It would be a shame to ruin a fantasy over something so petty."

"That would be a shame before God, Mr. Rousseau. Say so in the bible. I can show you. Hold on." I put a hand on the doorknob and he pounced up like a wolf after its meal and grabbed my arm.

"If you walk out this door, then you may as well walk out that other one too and not even bother to look back."

I looked him square in the face, in his eyes. He was serious. He was really about to make me do this. I bit the insides of my jaws to keep from telling him to take his little dick to hell and to fuck his mama while he was down there. He smiled, enjoying the moment.

"You don't have anywhere else to go. Said that yourself. Now go ahead and give me a taste of that chocolate."

I stared at him long enough for him to know that I hated him enough to wish death on him. He smiled wider and got back on the bed in the same position.

"Carry on." He rolled his fat finger. Lights. Camera. Action. He was the director and I was his actress. His hands slid down to the cocktail sausage up under his belly. His thighs looked like two pink, hairy pigs.

My mama used to poke me and my sister's belly after we finished eating. A tight stomach meant that you were full. His whole body looked full. His toes stretched and curled as he pulled on his dick. I could imagine God shaking his head in shame as He drew a neat little line through my name in the Good Book. I shut down my thoughts, or at least I tried to, and got onto the bed beside him. He rolled over on top of me and took my breath away. I didn't even fight for it back. I just prayed that he would smother me into an eternal, cold darkness.

I milked Mr. Rousseau for as long as I could. Then, I started showing. It wasn't his though. I knew that much by the way the baby was kicking. I had to be about six months in already. The red-faced bastard wasn't taking any chances though. He got the pissy-pants and took off. He even had the nerve to send the police by to escort me off the property. Talking about I hadn't paid in over three months. Oh, I paid alright. I didn't put up a fight though. I just left.

Luckily, I'd been saving the little lagniappe that he would give me outside of the grocery money. So when Jewel pointed out a new place for me, I had the money to claim it. I'd originally planned to use it to get rid of the baby, but something wouldn't let me do it. So I'd decided, instead, to give the child up after I had it.

I tell you no lie, that baby came out as fat and cute as she wanted to be. You know how most babies come out hollering, covered in white paste, and have a cone shaped head? Not her. She had a head full of jet black hair, was the color of pecan pie, my favorite, and just as sweet. She didn't even cry. The child came out sucking her thumb. There was no way that I could've given her up.

So there I was: a single mother of not one, not two, not three, but four kids. Even in death, Walter still tried to keep a hold on me. The nurse asked me what I wanted to name her and I didn't have a clue. Walter had always named the kids. I asked her what she thought the baby's name should be and she said Annette. It meant "grace" and was the name that she'd given her daughter that died a few hours after being born. I waited a few hours to make sure I wasn't handing my child the same fate, and then I went ahead and signed Annette on the certificate.

Unlike the other three, Annette made my hair long and thick, cleared my skin up, filled my bra out, and rounded my hips perfectly. I looked better after her than I did before having any of my kids. I couldn't keep a man out of my face. Messing around with more than one is what ended up getting my ass handed to me.

I had an old, bone-thin, raggedy mouth yellow man that was married with kids on the one hand and a tall, dark, and handsome thing with a million dollar smile and no attachments on the other hand. Problem was, raggedy mouth Earl had all the money and Jack, with the million dollar smile, had none. Earl was a big man in the shrimping industry and Jack was just one of the men who would go down to the dock every morning in hopes of getting some work.

Jack Johnson, named after the famous boxer. I loved me some Jack Johnson, but I couldn't let him stay with me. Walter scarred me for life. I vowed to never live with another man. I can do bad by my damn self, but to be honest with you, I wasn't doing bad for myself at all. As a matter of fact, bad wasn't nowhere in my vocabulary.

Everybody had that one year that was incomparable to any other. It's the year that made you feel like you were on top of the world and nothing was too far out of reach. 1965 was mine. The twins were five, Annette was three, and Doris was seven, meaning that she was finally old enough to watch her sisters when I needed to step out. And boy was I stepping out! Earl bought me my first car: a brand spanking new, all-white, Plymouth convertible. That car had white folk breaking their necks to see who was inside.

We lived in the cutest little cottage out in Gentilly Terrace, which was about the fanciest neighborhood that a colored family could live in New Orleans at that time. I even had a nanny. She kept the kids for me from the time I woke up until the sun started to set. During that time, me and Jewel would be out spending money like it grew on trees. Maison Blanche, D.H. Holmes, Godchaux's, and Gus Mayer were a few of our favorites, to a name a few. I could hardly pronounce most of the stores I spent money in and the white folk working there damn sure didn't like to see me in there.

Jewel was like a local celebrity. She'd gotten a small role in a film about the burlesque and had The Black Cat packed every night. That's exactly where I intended to be one Friday night after an eight-hour shift of shopping. I'd found the sexiest royal blue, scoop-neck, knee-length dress to wrap my curves and couldn't wait to show it off.

I was inside, warning Doris to hurry up and do something with them whining as twins before I got my belt and got to passing out ass whoopings. I couldn't find my other pearl earring to save my life and was about to ruin my stockings looking for it. I heard a honking outside. I looked out the window and sure enough, it was the taxi. *Dammit.*

"You look pretty, Mommy," Annette said, smiling.

"Thank you, baby." I reached down and kissed her on the cheek, and then wiped away the red print that my lipstick left. "Now go run out there and tell Auntie Jewel that Mama'll be out in a second."

"Okay," she said, skipping away.

"Mama, 'Nette running in the house!" Mona, one of the twins, ratted.

"If I needed your report, I'da asked for it. Now get out my room," I hissed.

I gave up on finding my other pearl and I damn sure wasn't about to do no fake jewelry. Once you get ahold of some real pearls, ain't no going back to the plastic ones. I pinned the curls on my left side back behind my ear and let the ones on the right side cover my right ear. It didn't look bad either. I spritzed my perfume behind both ears, on both wrists, between my cleavage, and between my thighs. I winked at the beauty looking back at me in the mirror and hurried on to that cab before I got left.

"Where to tonight, Precious Jewels?" The driver asked Jewel, calling her by her stage name.

"The Black Cat."

"I would've guessed The 500 Club by now."

"Not just yet. We'll be there before you know it, though."

He winked at her through the rearview mirror. Club 500 was the top club in New Orleans. Everybody that was a somebody frequented Club 500. The line of patrons stretched down Bourbon Street every night. Whenever stars visited the city, they partied at the 500 and stayed a few blocks down at the Roosevelt Hotel.

"What act you performing tonight?" I asked.

"I can't tell. Otherwise you might jump up there and do it before me," she said, smiling.

"Yeah. Right."

"You should, really."

"No way am I jumping on stage and stripping in front of a club full of gawking men."

"It's not stripping. It's dancing. The art of burlesque."

"Fancy it how you wanna, but I know what it is."

We pulled up to the corner of Bourbon and Royal. Jewel reached for my hands. All three of us held hands and bowed our heads. Jewel led us in prayer.

"Glorious St. Joseph, model all of those who are devoted to labor, obtain for me the grace to work conscientiously. To work above all, with purity of intention, and with detachment from self. All for Jesus, all for Mary, and all after you O Father Joseph. Such shall be my motto in life and death. Amen."

"Amen," the driver and I said in unison, lifting our heads. He got out and opened the door for us. Jewel slid out first and then me.

"You gotta be kidding me," I said.

"Don't worry. It looks empty now, but it'll be full by the time I'm on stage," she said, smiling and waving.

"I ain't talking about that. I'm talking about a whore praying for her performance."

"I'm not a whore, I'm a bur—"

"I know. You a burlesque dancer," I said, laughing.

"You ought to spend more time in prayer and less time in sin."

I cleared my throat. "What do you expect God to say? 'Jewel, my daughter. You've done well. You executed the talents I laid before you.'" I busted out laughing.

"You haven't been a saint yourself lately now, have you?" she asked.

We walked in the club through the back door, a black door. The entire right wall was a mirror station outlined in light bulbs with five rusted folding chairs. The marble countertop was covered in makeup, cocktail drinks, bobby pins, hot irons, and costume jewelry for days. Posters of famous nude black burlesque dancers covered the walls. Brassieres, panties, and high heels were strewn all over the floor.

A set of identical twins sat at the station. Dark skin girls. Both of them had finger-waves and were topless, wearing nothing but their underwear, stockings, and high heels, taking turns making up each other's faces. As if on cue, they both looked me up and down then went back to what they were doing.

Another woman, tall and lean, wore nothing at all. Even her boudoir was bare. She was scurrying around looking for something. "Excuse me," she said, kneeling down beside me. She'd found what she was looking for: the tiny back to an earring. She turned her smile to me.

Jewel took a spot in front of the mirror which was her second favorite place to be, next to church. She put her own makeup bag on the countertop next to a blue plastic basket full of sponges. I guess that was a minus as to being the only white dancer in the room. Come to think of it, she was probably the only white person in the club. She ain't even notice. Or if she did, she was good at making it seem that way.

Making sure to look at anything but the mirror, I watched everything around me. A poster of a topless Josephine Baker, with a long ponytail and a feather pouf behind her, made me sit with my back a little straighter. She started off eating out the garbage can and dancing on the street corner. Now everybody, especially white folk, loved her. *Imagine that.*

One of the girls smiled at me through the mirror. She was exceptionally pretty, having light skin, bright brown eyes, and freckles. I'd never seen a black girl with freckles before. Her short hair was curled tight and her necklace looked like a flattened chandelier.

A back corner of the room was shut off by a black curtain nailed to the ceiling. Toes and knees stuck out from the bottom of the curtain. The girl behind the curtain was obviously frustrated about something and was cussing up a storm.

"What's back there?" I asked Jewel.

"Where?" she asked, looking around through the mirror.

I pointed to the black curtain. She waved her hand, beckoning for me to come close. I leaned in.

"It's where the girls cram sponges up their privates when their cycle is running instead of having the decency to take a week off. Disgusting, right?" she whispered.

I felt my stomach turn and my face flush. "Disgusting ain't the word. I'm going outside for a minute," I said. She giggled.

"Make sure you're back in time for my show, witch!" she yelled.

Without looking back, I gave her two thumbs up. The twins, on cue, looked me up and down as I walked back past them. They whispered amongst themselves. I kept walking. I could really give a damn what anyone had to say about me.

The cool air felt good on my warm, flushed face. The night life was where I belonged, but I couldn't help feeling like I was sneaking, considering that I'd told Earl that I was visiting family back at home to keep him away for the night. I kept looking over my shoulder.

"Excuse me," I said to the crippled man that I bumped into.

He staggered and I grabbed both of his hands to keep him from falling. His palms felt cold and hard. He leaned in close to my ear before I got a chance to see his face. He smelled like a handful of mothballs, causing me to hold my breath to keep from gagging.

"I guess you free now, huh?"

I jumped back. It was Walter. Looking exactly the way he did, wearing the same clothes and all, as the day that he died. I opened my mouth to scream, but nothing came out. All it did was knock the breath out of my body. I tried to move, but couldn't. Wide awake, in the middle of Bourbon Street, I'd been hagridden.

I heard the sound of horses galloping behind me. I turned around and moved out of the way just in time before getting trampled. The trance had been broken. I turned around to see where he had gone, but he wasn't there. I looked all around me, into the dozes of smiling and laughing faces, but he wasn't there. He was gone.

I picked up my pace, looking over my shoulder every now and then. I shivered, knowing that he could appear at any moment from anywhere. *I don' lost my damn mind.* I kept running, back to the club. Straight there, no turns, no stops. I ran back in through the same back door. It slammed behind me. The girls all stopped to stare. I held my breath so no one would notice my labored breathing. One of the twins stood up, shaking her head.

"You gotta go! That's exactly why we ain't supposed to have visitors back here now," she said.

The girl with freckles stood up. "At least ask her if she's ok."

"And if she ain't? I guess we're supposed to protect her from whatever she running from out there."

"Why you have to be so rude, Rose?" Freckles asked.

"It's Mary," The twin replied. The other twin, Rose, laughed.

As much as I despised Mary at that moment, I could attest to the annoyance of being confused with your twin sister. It happened to me and Etta all the time and I was the only one who seemed annoyed by it. Etta, on the other hand, thought it was cute. Now, I was doing the same thing to my own twins.

"I'm fine. Thanks for asking," I said, looking at Mary.

Jewel was nowhere to be found in the dressing room, meaning that she must have been performing.

Freckles touched me lightly on the arm. Her touch warmed me. "You sure?" she asked. I nodded and walked up the stairs to the club.

I'd already missed her performance. She was bowing and the audience was clapping, whistling, and cheering. Jewel met me at the bottom of the stairs and hugged me. Her forehead was sweating and I had to back away from her before she rubbed her glitter and sweat off on me. The twins were making their way up to go on next and Freckles slid past me to go down the hall.

"Break a leg twins," Jewel said.

"Wouldn't you just love that," they said at the same time.

Jewel laughed.

"How do you like the girls?" she asked.

I shrugged. "Girls will be girls."

"Good. You'll work here with me then," she said, catching her breath.

"I don't exactly think you have the authority to make that call."

"Nope, but I know who do," she said, taking my hand and led me down a narrow hallway to another black door. Jewel knocked. No response. She knocked harder.

"Wait a got damn minute," the woman on the other side of the door yelled. "Knocking on my motha fucking door like you got damn crazy," she mumbled.

I heard the taps of her cane hitting the floor. She opened the door with a frown on her face. Freckles walked out of the office, looking like she'd been sent to bed without eating. Delores stared at her hind side until she was no longer in sight. I looked back to see what she was looking at. I turned back around and could've sworn I saw Delores lick her lips.

"Come on in and shut the door behind you," Delores said, walking back to her chair. She sat down and handed Jewel her cane. The folded table in front of her was covered in money. More money than I had ever seen at one time in my life. A brown envelope sat at the corner of the table. The space before her was cleared off. Three other chairs sat at the opposite end of the table. One of them pulled out from where Freckles sat. I guessed that she was in there counting money. *Now that's where I'm trying to be.* I felt Delores' piercing grey eyes staring at me. Embarrassed, I looked away. She smiled, revealing her gold trimmed teeth.

"Delores, do you kiss your mama with that nasty mouth of yours?" Jewel asked.

"You knocked on my door. I opened it. Whatchu want?"

"Well my friend, Louisa, here need a job. And quick. She—"

"She dumb?"

"No I ain't dumb."

"Well you don't need nobody talking for you then," she said and looked up at Jewel.

She patted my shoulder. "I'll be outside in the taxi waiting."

I nodded my head, when I actually wanted to beg her not to leave me in this room with this manly looking woman staring at me like this. The door shut behind Jewel and Delores leaned back as if she'd been waiting on Jewel to leave so she could relax.

"So, you need work?"

I cleared my throat. "Yes."

"Who was that chasing you?"

"Umm, uh, nobody."

The question was a curveball. It caught me off guard. How was I supposed to tell her that my dead husband had shown up and shown out in the middle of Bourbon Street? Of all the lies that I'd ever used about my black eyes and blue bruises, I couldn't think of one lie for the life of me.

She held up her hand. Each finger on her hand had at least two rings on it and her wrist wore a heavy gold watch that was made for a man.

"One thing I can't stand is a liar. If you lie to me, you'll steal from me too." She stared at me without blinking. I swallowed the thick ball of anxiety in the back of my throat. "Is that understood?"

"Yes."

"If it's none of my business, then say so, but don't lie. Ever."

I nodded my head. I was beginning to feel like I was at my mama's house again. The conversation was quickly beginning to climb on top of my nerves.

Chapter 6

T hat blind boy—Ray Charles, I think his name is—had a new song called "Crying Time." I went out in the cold, night air with wet hair wrapped around small pink sponges, a big ol' pregnant belly, and house shoes to buy that record with one of the last few dollars that I had to my name. It was my theme song for 1966. 1965 might've been my year to climb, but the following was my year to fall.

I wasn't so upset about being pregnant that time around. That baby was an investment. Delores had been getting on my last damn nerve, but I couldn't seem to find a job anywhere else in the city. That had a lot to do with the fact that I didn't have any experience in doing anything. The only jobs going for black women during that time was either cleaning white folk's houses, styling other black women's hair, teaching, or nursing. Cleaning white folk's houses also meant taking care of their kids. I barely wanted my own, so I damn sure wasn't about to be raising nobody else's. I was pretty good at setting my own hair, but when it came to somebody else's then I was out of my range. Teaching and nursing required education and mine stopped a few years too early; so that was off limits. The only thing left to do was to show a little leg.

I knew men didn't sneak behind their old ladies back to go run behind some old chicken. No, they wanted some young, tender meat. Since I wasn't getting any younger, I went ahead and kept the baby. That meant that I had to get rid of Jack so there wouldn't be any confusion. That was Earl's baby and if it wasn't, then I made it like it was. One thing about Earl, he took care of his kids. Rumor was: he had more than fifteen of them running around the city. I didn't give a damn though. Mine was about to make sixteen.

He was something happy too. You would've thought the man didn't have any kids. I knew that wasn't true though because he had two boys and a little girl with his wife. He called every five minutes to make sure that I took my vitamins and made it to my doctor's appointments. I knew that baby would be something spoiled because the only time that I went to the doctor with my other ones was to have them. He was putting money in my hand quicker than I could get rid of it and need I remind you that I spent fast? He would also pop up at all times of day to come rub my feet and my belly.

That's who I figured it had to be when somebody went to banging on my door like they were crazy. I was in the middle of polishing my fingers. I stormed up front, opened the door, and slammed it back.

"Please."

"Gone on from round here now, Jack!" I yelled through the door.

"I miss you. I just had to see you," he said.

"You seen me. Now gone," I warned.

"Just open the door. All I need is five minutes. Tops."

I shouldn't have opened the damn door. I should not have opened that damn door. What did I do though? I opened the damn door.

"You got five minutes," I said, looking down at my wrist.

His eyes travelled down to my stomach and locked.

"Louisa, you ain't tell me I had a baby on the way." He looked up at me with tears in his eyes. "Why? Why didn't you tell me?"

I took a deep breath and shut the door behind him. I couldn't just throw him out. I felt that I owed him some kind of apology.

Once upon a time, I did love the man—sort of. I plopped down on the couch and patted the seat next to me. He sat beside me.

"I enjoyed the time that we spent together," I said.

"I did too. I swear I did. I think about it all the time."

Rena and Mona came running up front. They saw him and screamed "Uncle Jack" while running for his lap. He smiled and lifted them both up into the air before bringing them back down onto his knees.

"Y'all gone back to the room. Grown folks talking," I said.

They turned their bottom lips down which only made them look worse since Rena looked like her pajamas had cereal for breakfast instead of her and Mona's little nappy ass pigtails were standing up all over her head. I had a good mind to whoop both of their little asses, but I didn't. That time.

"Now what were we saying?" I asked, redirecting my attention to Jack.

He shook his head and placed a hand on my stomach. "How far along are you?"

"Doctor said it'll be here in another two months," I answered.

"It's not too late for us to get married, you know?"

I moved his hand from my stomach. "That's not where my heart at."

"Well I'ma be a part of my child's life regardless."

"It ain't yours."

"Like hell it ain't," he said, standing to his feet. "As many dreams as I've been having, waking up sick every morning. You'd think I was carrying the baby."

"Oh shit, I forgot your people fool with that voodoo mess."

"It ain't voodoo and that ain't got nothing to do with this," he said, pointing to my stomach. "This is about me and my seed."

"How much money you got in your pocket?" I asked.

He looked confused. "What that got to do with anything?"

"Answer the question," I demanded.

"None," he said, shrugging. "But I've been getting a good bit of work down at the dock."

"And where you staying at?"

"With one of the other workers and his wife right now," he answered.

I shook my head. "That's exactly my point. You ain't got a pot to piss in or a window to throw it out of. Yet, you in here talking about being somebody daddy."

"My mama and daddy raised all seven of us in a one bedroom shack with holes in the roof. Some days we ain't even have food to fill our bellies, but we made it. We might not have had much, but—"

"Did you just hear yourself? Who wanna live like that? Not me! Now look here, you might not want to hear this, but you need to. I got four kids back there and another one up in me. My rent cost more than you made all year. Now, I loved you and I believe you when you say that you loved me too, but love don't pay no bills. I got to do what I got to do to make the best life that I can for me and my kids. If you care anything about us, then you'll walk right back out that door and not come back."

Before he could respond, someone started banging at the door. Since we were sitting right in the front room, it sounded louder than usual. My heart sunk and for a second, I was paralyzed. I knew, without a shadow of a doubt, who it was that time.

"Gone out the back door," I whispered to Jack.

"I'm a man. What I look like running?" he yelled. His nostrils flared and his fists balled at his sides. I would've called him on the shit, but it was no time to be arguing.

"Louisa, open up this door before I mess my pants," Earl yelled through the door.

"Jack, please leave," I begged, still whispering. I locked my fingers together in prayer and was one second away from getting down on my knees. The bastard wasn't budging though.

Then the door opened.

"What the he—"

"Mr. Earl?"

"Louisa, he had better be some kind of kin to you," Earl said, looking Jack up and down.

"No sir, but I am some kin to that baby she carrying," Jack answered, sticking his chest out.

"Earl, the boy just talking crazy. Jack gone on home," I said, trying to kill the fire before it spread.

"To what baby?" Earl asked, pushing me aside.

"You heard me right. That one right there."

"Look'a here lil' nigga. I don't take too kind to bullshit. You understand me?" Earl asked. His chest was pressed right up against Jack's. Jack wasn't backing down. My living room was starting to feel real small and my belly was starting to feel bigger than what it was.

Doris ran out from the back room, saying that somebody had said something, but I didn't really hear her. I just told her to gone back to her room until I said to come out. She looked up at both men, back at me, and then grabbed her sisters, who had followed her. Their room door shut and locked. I turned my attention back to my living room which was about to be a boxing ring if I didn't do something quick.

"I don't give a damn who you are!" Jack yelled.

"You ain't gotta give a damn. My pistol will give one for you."

"That 'posed to scare me? Huh?" Jack asked. Spit was flying out of his mouth and his eyes had turned fire red. I was getting scared for Earl. He was much shorter, smaller, and older than Jack. One punch and he would be out cold.

"Louisa, you better make some sense of this here and quick too. Else it's gon' be some bloodshed up in here," Earl warned.

"Ain't no sense to make of it, Earl. You this baby's father. That's all there is to it. Now Jack, if you don't leave from here, I'ma go get Earl's pistol my damn self."

Jack stared at me, not saying anything. His nostrils were still flared and his chest was heaving as if he'd just finished running over here. He took a deep breath that exhaled kind of ragged then said, "You can have it. She ain't worth it, not that I could afford her anyway. Like she said, her rent probably cost more than I don' made all year and obviously you the one paying it. I'll let y'all get back to being a happy family." He stared me down for another few seconds, long enough to feel like hours, and then left.

"And don't bother to show up at my dock tomorrow," Earl yelled behind him.

The screen door slammed shut and the room fell silent. Earl took a seat on the sofa and I just stood there, not really knowing what to do or say. What I really wanted was to rewind time, follow my first mind, and not open the door for Jack.

"Get me a beer," he said.

I hurried off to the kitchen to get it. I popped the top and brought it out to him. It was ice cold already, but I still ran back to the kitchen to fix him a cup of ice just in case. I brought it back and set it on the table in front of him. He took a long swig from the bottle, stopped to belch, and then finished it off.

"You still got yo' job down there at Delores'," he asked.

"Not right now, I don't. Not until after I have the baby," I answered, wondering how in the hell he even found that out. I never once told him that I was working.

"Whose baby is it?"

"Yours," I answered quickly.

He snorted. "You sound more sure than you act. Tell the truth. Them kids' daddy ain't run off. Did he? You probably couldn't point him out in a zoo full of animals."

"Don't do me that Earl. I ain't never tell you no lie. He ran off and left us right after I had my fourth baby girl, Annette. That's the honest to God truth," I lied.

"Girl, you wouldn't know the truth if it bit you in the ass. I ain't got the time to sort through your lies. I got a whole family at the house."

"What you saying, Earl?" I asked.

"I'm saying that when I met you, you was so broke that your ass had to borrow tears just to cry. You get a little something and don't know how to act. Just like a typical nigga. So guess what?"

"Come on Earl. Don't be like that. What about the baby? What about me and the girls? We can't make it without you, Earl." I started to cry. I felt like Cinderella at midnight. The floor was sinking beneath my feet, my clothes were going ragged, the jewelry was melting from my body, and my belly was going hungry again.

"It's too late for all that, baby. Save them tears. You gon' need 'em," he said, digging into his back pocket. He pulled out a wad of cash, peeled a few bills off, and folded them into the palm of my hand. "This should last you until you start working again."

And that was it. He left. I knew he wasn't coming back. I didn't try to beg him because well, I knew that it was nothing that I could say to make him come back. Once again, I was assed-out. I counted the twenty dollar bills in my hand. They amounted to $200. Since I never had to concern myself with the rent, I didn't even know how much it was. That also meant that I didn't even know where to go to find out. I just had to wait until the first and hope, pray, and wish that it wouldn't be all that I had.

It turned out not to be all of my money, but it was damn near. I could've cried when that man came to the door talking about rent was $125. Tears wouldn't solve nothing, so I just went ahead and made plans to make our next move.

Out of desperation, I applied to all the public housing projects, but was turned down each time. The only one that had space available was the Fischer Projects that had just opened up on the West Bank. I stood in a line longer than Mahalia Jackson's second line, in the freezing cold, for more than four hours, with four kids, a big belly, and swollen ankles.

It finally got to be my turn. The lady asked where I currently lived. I gave her my address. She looked up at me and asked if I was married or single. I told her that I was widowed.

"How much cash do you have? That includes in the bank, in your home, and in your purse."

"Not a dollar," I answered.

She turned up her mouth as if I were getting on her last damn nerve. Rena was crying and had snot bubbling down her nose. I wiped it with her shirt, picked her up, and began bouncing her on my hip.

"Where are you employed?" she asked.

"Nowhere," I responded.

"Well how do you afford to live in Gentilly Terrace, Ms. Williams?"

"Gifts."

"Gifts from where?" she asked.

"From whichever man that I'm sexing. That's where," I answered.

Her eyebrows shot up. "Well we are currently only taking applications from those in emergency situations and—"

"Ma'am. I just paid rent with my last bit of money. Next month this time, me and my girls will be sleeping under a bridge somewhere."

"Like I said, We. Are. Only. Taking. Applications. From. Those. In. Emergency. Situations," she spelled out.

They had a few security guards standing by so instead of showing my ass, I readjusted Rena on my hip, grabbed Annette's hand, and told the rest of them to come on. I had to get out of there before I beat the cheap foundation off that woman's face.

I needed someone to talk to. I needed a friend. I needed my Jewel, but hadn't heard from her in months. I figured that she was just disgusted in me for being pregnant once again. I could hardly blame her. If I were in her shoes, I would think the same thing. The last time that I talked to her, she was moving out of her place. She'd finally got hired down at The 500 Club and said that the manager took interest in the girls' lives in and out of the club. He didn't like where she was staying and suggested that she move if she planned to continue dancing there.

Her new place was nice, real nice, from the outside. I never got to do nothing more than peek inside. Even then, she looked all nervous like somebody was coming for her. Hell, she was starting to scare me. She wouldn't even let the kids hug her.

"Somebody after you?" I asked.

"Uh, no. Well, not really, but, um…I think you'd better go."

"Well what about my question? Can me and the girls stay here for a month or two, or not? You know I wouldn't be asking if I didn't have to."

"I don't think that would be a good idea."

"Scared your new manager gon' find out?" I joked.

"Exactly. He isn't too fond of…of…of, people like you. I mean, you know that I don't care, but yeah. He said it's bad for business and…I don't know. This has always kind of been my dream, you know?"

I couldn't believe what I was hearing, but I nodded anyway. "Yeah, it makes sense Jewel. It makes perfect sense."

I couldn't find anywhere else to stay. I had just enough money to pay for the next month's rent, but that didn't include the water or light bill. Walter had burned most of my bridges to smoldering ash so my options for shelter were extremely limited. Thank God for President Johnson and his new food stamp program. Else, me and my kids would have starved to death.

A few days later, my water broke. It was more than a month too soon, but the doctor didn't try to stop it. I was in labor for more than thirteen hours and my blood pressure shot up so high that I bled from my fingernails. They said that I almost died and I remember praying on more than one occasion that God would go ahead and take me. Or at least, take the baby for causing me so much hell. He granted neither of the two wishes, leaving me with yet another girl—my fifth one.

Charity Hospital was just beginning to desegregate so that was my first time having a white staff deliver one of my kids. My nurse looked just like the woman in that cooking spray commercial. When she asked me what I wanted to name her, I could not have possibly cared less. I asked her what she thought that the name should be.

"That's not in my job description. I have three more women down the hall in the same position as you. So I'm going to have to ask you to make it quick."

"Pam!" I said, remembering the name of the spray in the commercial.

"Pam it is," she said, then handed me the birth certificate to sign.

Chapter 7

I 'll be damned if Pam didn't come out looking just like Earl's ugly ass. I threw her in the stroller one morning and caught two buses to get down to the dock and show him. He looked at her, back up at me, lit a cigarette, and said congratulations. I went so far as to tell him that he didn't even have to come around if he didn't want to. Just send some money by for the baby. He had the nerve to tell me that he didn't take care of other people's baby.

"She is yours, Earl," I said, standing with my hand on my hip.

"Until you can get me some proof, I'ma have to ask you to leave from my place of business."

My life was shot to shit. Earl had the car towed away in the middle of the night. Delores didn't want my "fat ass" working in her club. I had to give up my nice house for a two-bedroom, one-bathroom apartment. Imagine that with five kids. Although I didn't have any rent to pay, I wouldn't dare call it a blessing. The neighbors living above us had heavy ass feet and did a bunch of partying and fighting. On top of that, every time they turned on their tub faucet, water leaked down into my kitchen. Below our apartment lived an old ass woman that banged on our ceiling with her broom whenever she heard the slightest noise. As if that weren't enough, another old hag, Ms. Mae, lived beside me and felt it her duty to tell me how to raise my damn kids. I told her more than once that if she thought she could do better, she was more than welcome to have all five of them.

The only time that I left the house was to go to the liquor store for a six-pack of Jax beer and a pint of gin. If it wasn't that, then I was going down to the welfare office to explain why I still needed free rent, free groceries, and a measly ass welfare check each month. Having to do all that explaining was a new thing, so the other women in the apartment building said. The government changed the programs' letters from AFDC to TANF and claimed that it gave them the right to dig even deeper in your business: Are you on drugs? How many alcoholic beverages do you consume per day? How many jobs did you apply to this month? How many visitors did you have in your house this month? How long did they stay? Are your kids going to school regularly?

I answered the sickening questions so that I could continue my life as a drunk ass couch potato. Every morning, if it was the last thing I did, I made sure them kids went to school. If it wasn't for Pam, I would have the whole house to myself, but she wasn't nothing but two. She wasn't so bad though. She didn't say much of nothing unless she was hungry. Other than that, she just sat there looking dumb as dirt.

In the mornings, I fixed us bowls of grits and sausage. Then it was to the couch, for me, with my can of beer and newspaper. Some hippie, white boy delivered a NOLA Express every morning. It didn't talk about much, mainly about the war. I would flip through it then stash it under the couch for when we had seafood. After reading the paper, it was TV time. I only watched channel four. Everything else showing on the television was supposed to be funny and I wasn't much in the laughing mood in them days. I guess the news had a lot to do with that too.

For a while all they talked about was the Zodiac Killer—some murderer on the loose up in the California. Then it was on to the Vietnam War. Over 16,000 Americans had been killed and President Johnson was trying to send even more over there to perish. I liked to died when they announced that Martin Luther

King, Jr. was killed. I kept saying that I was going to make my way to at least one of his speeches. Needless to say, I never made it.

A few months later, the other Kennedy boy got killed. To me, that was the end of hope for black folk. Then, the Civil Rights Act went through which was supposed to make life for black folk better. I ain't never saw no difference for anybody anywhere. A few people in my building had the nerve to throw a party to celebrate the new law. I was getting off the bus, coming from my appointment down at the welfare office, when they asked me if I wanted to join them.

"For what?" I asked.

"To celebrate," they yelled.

"And just what are we supposed to be celebrating?" I asked. "Y'all fools still gon' be living in the projects, being fed with the same food stamps, and waiting on the same welfare check as me. Ain't shit changed. And you better hope this new son of a gun, Nixon, don't take that. From what I hear, black folk ain't much of his cup of tea."

I'm sure they talked shit behind my back, but I didn't stick around to hear it. I took the stairs on up to my second floor apartment. My neighbor, Ms. Mae, was sitting in front of her door eating crawfish. She offered the kids some. Doris, Reta, and Mona tried to run over there to get some. I yanked their little asses back by their collars and pushed them in the house.

"God don't like ugly," she tsked.

"Yeah, He don't like a lot of things—especially black folk and nosey neighbors."

She shook her head while sucking the head of the crawfish. She dropped the red shell into a plastic bag and then reminded me that I would have to answer to God one day. "The Good Book says that no man knows the day or time, but He coming back."

"Ain't nobody coming nowhere and you know why? Because God is right here," I said, pointing to my chest. "If I want a blessing, then I'll get up and get a job. If I want to create life, then I'll spread my legs. If I want to end life, then I can do that too."

I left her outside, rambling about something or another, and went inside and shut my door. She had pissed me off. I locked the door behind me and took my brown paper bag out of my purse.

"Mama, why we couldn't eat crawfish with Auntie Mae?" Reta asked.

"That ain't your damn aunt. Now go run y'all some bath water," I answered, untwisting the top to my bottle of gin.

"We hungry, Mama," Mona whined.

"Yeah, we hungry, Mama," Annette joined in.

"Doris, fix these damn kids something to eat before I lose my mind up in here." I plopped down on the sofa and took a gulp from the bottle. I squeezed my eyes shut from the burn going down my throat and settling into my belly.

"Yes ma'am and when I'm finished, can I go outside?"

"I'll think about it. Now come turn on this TV. Reta go run y'all some bath water, I said!"

"But you said that we could eat first."

"Lord have mercy. Doris, fix the kids something to eat!" I yelled.

"Yes ma'am."

I took another swig, laid down, and closed my eyes. I began counting down the seconds until the kids were washed up, in the bed, and out of my face. I felt someone tapping my leg and opened my eyes. It was Pam with her lip poked out.

"Eat eat," she cried.

"Doris!" I yelled.

The floor began thumping which was our signal to quiet down. She had picked the wrong day. I jumped up from the couch and began stomping my foot in the same spot. She banged at her roof again. I stomped again. She stopped, meaning that she must've gotten the point.

Doris was holding her hands over her mouth to stop herself from laughing. I brushed past her, snatched the half done grilled cheese sandwiches off the stove, tore it, and gave half to Pam and the other half to Annette.

"Now hurry up and fix them other ones a sandwich before I have all y'all sleeping outside tonight," I threatened.

"Yes, ma'am," she answered.

I went and sat back on the couch.

"Mama," Doris asked softly.

"What?"

"When I'm finished, can I go outside?"

"Doris, I don't care."

"Can we go outside too, Mama?" Mona asked, whining of course.

"Yes. Go and don't come back," I answered.

"Mama, can we go live with our daddy?" Annette asked.

"We ain't got no daddy 'Nette. Him dead," Reta answered.

"'Nette ain't got the same daddy as us. Her got her own daddy," Mona said to Reta.

"Not aaah! Pam the only one with her own daddy," Reta answered.

They had another ten seconds before I was getting up off the couch and going to get my belt. Lucky for them, Doris walked out the kitchen with a plate stacked with sandwiches. She gave Reta the one with no crust, Mona's looked like it had been cooked a little longer, and the one she took a bite of was oozing with cheese. They ate and left, taking their two little sisters with them.

I cut the TV on and took a few gulps from the bottle while Tom Fears, the coach of the city's new football team, talked about his plans for the upcoming season. He had Walter Roberts, one of the few black players on the team, standing next to him. His little young, fine self reminded me how long it had been since I'd been with a man. I took a few more swigs during the commercial break and by that time, my throat was numb. I was drinking that gin like water and it took some work to focus on the TV. Knowing my limit, I screwed the cap back on the bottle and stuffed it under the couch pillow.

After the commercial break, the news came back on showing some jazz players. They were blowing it down too, getting ready for some big festival to celebrate the city's 250th year anniversary. Louis Armstrong and a few other big names that I didn't recognize were supposed to be there. The trumpet players had always been my favorite. They had a natural rhythm and arrogance to them that just twisted my panties in all kinds of knots.

That little five-minute news story had me sitting up and thinking. I had to get my life together. I couldn't spend the rest of my life on that broken down couch in that broken down apartment. I had to get out and get my shine back. I had to get to that festival, but first I needed something to wear. All of my good clothes fit the old me. Since I'd just gotten my check, I had a couple of dollars to my name. Not much, but I could work it. I wobbled my drunk behind off the couch, slipped my shoes on, and was out the door.

"Just as drunk as the sky is blue. Need to be ashamed of yourself," Ms. Mae said, shaking her head.

I almost tripped and fell on my face trying to shoo her away. I made my way down the two flights of stairs and headed east toward Marais Street so that I wouldn't have to pass the cemetery. Canal wasn't nothing but a ten-minute walk from where we lived.

"Mama, where you going?" one of the twins asked. I couldn't tell which one it was.

"None of your business. That's where. Y'all got another thirty minutes out here and I want everybody washed and in the bed," I yelled without looking back.

By the time that I made it to Canal, I was just about sobered up. I took a cheap bottle of perfume out of my purse and spritzed myself so that I wouldn't be walking around them people stores smelling like a mix of liquor and sweat.

I had to let the street car pass before I could cross and then almost got hit by a hippie riding a bicycle. I gave him a good cussing. He held up his little peace sign and kept going. I nearly tripped over a girl sitting down on the sidewalk. I had to grab the wall for balance.

"You have some change to spare?" she asked.

Her voice sounded so familiar. I cocked my head to the side to get a good look at her and realized that it was Freckles from down at the Black Cat. She looked so different without the makeup and costume. She wasn't dirty, but she was definitely smaller than I remembered and was wearing some cut-up jeans and an oversized white t-shirt.

"Girl what you doing out here?" I asked.

"Louisa?"

"Get up from that ground like that. What happened to you?"

"Life," she said then dropped her arms down at her sides.

I invited her to tag along and while we walked, we caught up. She explained what was really going down in the office between she and Delores all that time. It made me sick to my stomach. She later met a man at the club who swept her off her feet, out of the club's doors for good, and into her own home. They traveled and the poor girl thought she was in love until one day he just stopped calling and coming around. Left her high and dry.

"You couldn't find another friend?" I asked her.

"Another friend for what? My heart was still, well still is, with him," she sulked.

I kept my opinions to myself. I found a nice little peach colored dress in one of the department stores. It ate up all but five dollars of my check, but it was worth it to me. It was A-lined so it pushed my ladies up real nice and flowed around the parts that I didn't care to show off. Though Freckles said that she liked it, I could tell that she was a bit jealous. She probably thought that I was the same Louisa that she'd met before. I didn't offer much of myself to her though. I just told her that I'd had another baby and left it at that.

"So how many is that now?" she asked.

"Five."

"You look really good to have five kids," she said, stopping at the same corner that I'd found her on.

"You sleep out here?" I asked.

"Yeah... well, not really...not here, no."

"Get your stuff and come on."

"Where we going?" she asked, as if she had something better to do.

"You coming to stay with me until you get back on your feet."

Chapter 8

I'd met a man down at the jazz festival that I had gone to. His name was Conti. He couldn't keep his eyes off of me. His stare had me feeling real nervous. I was brushing stuff off of my dress that wasn't even there and making sure my hair was still in place. I felt like a teenager all over again, like I didn't have five kids waiting for me back at the house. Crazy part is, he wasn't even all that handsome and he was short.

"You are so beautiful," he said. His accent made my knee joints loosen up.

"Thank you," I said, pretending that I wasn't much interested.

"Are you here alone?"

"Maybe. Maybe not. Why? What tricks you hiding up them sleeves?" I asked.

"No tricks," he said, holding his hands up. "Only I see a beautiful woman and desire her company. If she's not already spoken for, that is."

"Where you from?"

He smiled. "Ghana."

"Where?"

"Africa. West Africa."

"And I'm just s'posed to believe that you came all the way to America to stand in front of me like you ain't never seen no woman before."

He didn't respond. He just stood there with a big ass grin on his face. Over time, I'd come to learn that that meant that he didn't comprehend what I'd said. His eyes had a sparkle to them that set off his smile and made me notice that he had the best set of lips that I'd ever seen on a man before. He was chocolate just the way that I liked my men and had shoulders that looked like he could prop me up on them and carry me for miles. He stood with his head high and chest out. I was always tempted to push him, just to see if he would budge though I knew that he wouldn't.

"What is your name?" he asked.

"Louisa," I answered.

"Louisa," he repeated and then kept repeating like he was trying to taste it. Then after saying it about four or five times, he smiled like it must have tasted good to him or something.

He told me his name and then started talking about something or another. I know that because his mouth was moving, but I wasn't hearing anything that he was saying. I couldn't get past my thoughts and the pulling at the center of my chest. What is he doing to me? He don't even know me. Out of all these women out here, he can't possibly be stuck on me.

"I got kids back at home. Five of 'em," I said, interrupting him.

He didn't mind that I had kids. He wouldn't quit bothering me about meeting them for a good long while. I wasn't in the same rush though. After a few months, I finally came around and introduced them. Conti didn't have a whole lot of money, but he had enough. He would take me out to the show, out to eat, on picnics, give the girls gifts every now and then, and all kinds of nice little things like that.

I must have come home from the festival smiling or humming, because Freckles—well, her real name was Alyson, but I preferred Freckles—picked up on it immediately. She was polishing Doris' fingernails, but stopped to tease me about meeting a man. I told her about him and then said that I was going to bed early. I wanted to hurry up and dream about him while he was still fresh on my mind. Freckles told me to go ahead and that she would take care of everything while I slept.

By that time, she should've been long gone. I surely didn't expect to still be living with another woman under my roof after a year, but Freckles wasn't so bad. She knew the procedure. If the caseworker popped up, then she was the babysitter, looking after the kids while I was out looking for a job. On top of that, she cleaned up behind herself, loved to cook, minded her own damn business, seemed to know when I didn't feel like being bothered, and even better—she loved them damn kids. That was right on time for me because I had begun spending more time with Conti.

The problems didn't arise until one evening when I came home early. I was supposed to sleep over at Conti's, but I was feeling a little under the weather. The kids were outside playing, which for one, it was too late for them to be out. It was going on eight o'clock at night and it was cold enough for me to see my breath. Since it was my house, I didn't knock on doors, I opened them. When I opened hers that night, I found her legs sky high and some man between them pounding away. They saw me and jumped up to cover themselves up, but it was too late.

He got dressed and left. He didn't think I saw him slip her the money, but I did. She didn't think that I saw her slip the money in her bra, but I did. She tried to lie and say it was her boyfriend, but couldn't even come up with a name. I reminded her that I wasn't her damn mama, but expected the truth since she was living up under my roof. She confessed that she'd been sleeping with men for a few dollars here and there in order to save enough money to get her own place. I reminded her of the risk that she was putting me and my kids in. We could've been evicted for that. If she were going to keep it up, then she was going to have to pay me for the trouble. She agreed.

Everything was going good after that. She respected my rules. I didn't want the men there unless the kids were outside and I wanted half of each payment. Between my welfare checks that came in twice a month and the money that she was handing over once or twice a week, I was doing alright for myself. I was able to start shopping and being a woman again. This time, I made sure that I saved first. I'd even stopped drinking and the pounds were dropping like flies.

I wanted to throw a nice little New Year's Eve celebration at the house and bought more food and liquor than I had room for. Conti brought over a few friends, Freckles invited two of hers, a few of the neighbors that I could tolerate came over, and that made a party. We ate good, drank good, laughed loud, danced, and acted like some damn fools. Everybody needed some of that in their life every now and then. It's good for the soul.

After the clock struck midnight, the champagne was gone, and the fireworks had finished lighting up the sky, I was ready to get laid. I told Freckles to clear the house out for me and that I would see her in the morning. She promised that she would and she did...kind of. The house was spic and span. You couldn't even tell that we'd had a party the night before except for the fact that one of the guests was still there.

Her name was Ann and was singing the same sad ass song that Freckles was. She'd followed a man down to New Orleans and got left high and dry. She ended up homeless which is where she met Freckles and was bouncing around from shelter to shelter. She was originally from Bossier City which was a hop and a skip away from where I was from, Coushatta. We didn't know each other, but after throwing around a few names, we knew a few of the same people. That's what led me to opening my home to her.

She did a few things for some change too, but she was upfront about hers. She told me that she would give me half of whatever she made and would be gone as soon as she had enough to make it on her own. I was hesitant at first, but I got to thinking about how much money I could make. I told them as long as they didn't have the men around my girls, handed me all of my money on time, and was gone by three months then it was fine by me. Both of them agreed.

I figured they had to have some dull snatch. Between the two of them, they couldn't afford a place to live. Weren't they sick of sleeping in the front room? Then again, Freckles was doing a lot of shopping and it wasn't long before Ann was shopping it up too. Hell, the three of us would go on splurges together sometimes. Ann was bringing in some serious change, but that also meant that she was bringing around a lot of men. I started getting nervous. I started shopping less and saving more. I only touched my savings twice. The first time was to buy a gun.

It wasn't too long after I bought it that I had to use it. I'd come in one morning after having been out all night with Conti. It was a Saturday, I remember. The kids were outside playing. I walked up the stairs, opened the front door, and found Ann getting her ass whooped by a big ole' black man and Freckles was huddled up in the corner like a scared cat. I took the gun out of my purse and told him to get the hell out of my house.

He smiled and started walking toward me. I could see it in his eyes then, that he was high on something. His mind wasn't right. I told him again to leave. Ann cried that he didn't pay her. I blocked the door and told him to pay the girl first. He ignored me, but kept walking toward me. I put my finger over the trigger like the man down at the gun shop taught me. He took another step and I shot at him, just missing his head, to show him that I wasn't playing.

He held up his hands over his head and started crying. I stepped closer, pressing the gun into his chest. Ann dug through his pockets, took his wallet out, and tossed it to Freckles. That fool counted out an even forty and tried to hand the wallet back to him.

I knocked it back to the floor and told him he was free to go, but if he ever came back, then he would be the second body on my list.

Not long after he left, the police showed up. They got a call that someone was shooting. I corrected them, that it was only one shot. I had to scare away a man that was trying to rob us. I don't even know where that lie came from. I didn't have time to make one up because I didn't give thought that they would come. The officers looked a little skeptical, but wrote up a little incident report anyway and left.

After that, the neighbors got to talking and the caseworker started doing more "random" visits. Refusing to take any more chances, I went ahead and got another place. After almost having to blow that nigga's head off, I knew it wouldn't be a good idea to bring the kids with us. Once the girls moved out, I was going to move the kids over into the new place.

That was the plan.

What ended up happening, however, was another girl named Paulette moving in. Paulette was kind of young. My guess was about sixteen—maybe seventeen. She was a pretty girl. Had some big ole' doe eyes, was forever grinning like everything was a joke, real skinny, and had some long, wavy hair like she was mixed with something somewhere down the line. She claimed to be nineteen going on twenty. That was the first telltale sign there. If you grown, then you grown; you ain't "going on" nothing. Since she was adding to the pot, I let her stay. I couldn't fathom how Freckles just so happened to be running into all these whores.

The money was coming in so fast; I was counting it about ten times a day just to make sure that I wasn't dreaming. I got to wishing the girls would just forget about my three-month rule. I must have wished upon the right star that night because they never left and the money kept rolling in. I came to learn, though, that with more money came more problems.

I was one person trying to divide myself three ways: with the girls, with Conti, and with my kids. The girls were grown and could take care of themselves. Problem was, whenever I wasn't there, I got to worrying about them stealing from me. Conti was getting suspicious, asking me who the other man was every five minutes. I loved him and enjoyed our time together, but all that questioning me was getting old.

Then with the kids, if it wasn't some mess with one, then it was the other. Doris had started her period and if she wasn't sucking her teeth and rolling her eyes at somebody then she was crying behind some foolishness. Reta didn't want to mind Doris no more. Mona had developed asthma. 'Nette was having nightmares and Pam was just Pam.

The straw broke the camel's back when Doris and Reta called themselves throwing down. They got to fighting and although I wasn't there, I would bet my last dollar that the other three got to crying and carrying on. One of the neighbors called the police and I was pulling up at the same time as they were. My explanation wasn't worth two nickels rubbed together that time because the Housing Authority told me to pack my shit and be out within 48 hours. That meant that I had to close shop and move the kids in until I could figure something out.

Freckles didn't have a problem with it. Paulette, her dingbat ass, befriended Doris like she was twelve instead of…however the hell old she was. Ann looked like she'd been fed a spoon of ashes. If her money wasn't coming like it was, I would've put her ass out of my house right there on the spot.

Not being able to come up with a better alternative and as much as I hated to do so, I needed my mama to keep the kids for a little while for me. I sent a letter and waited for almost a month, but no response. So, I called.

The line scratched static then cleared. "Hello?" She still sounded the same.

"Hello, Mama?" I instantly regretted saying it after I did, but it was too late to take it back. Plus, I had bigger fish to fry. "This Louisa."

"I know who this is."

"Did you get my letter?"

"Yeah, I got it," she answered.

"Well can they come? It's just for a month or two. Three at the most."

The phone clicked. The bitch had hung up in my damn face. I called back. She answered on the first ring. "If I wanted the nappy head heffas, don't you think I would've wrote you back? Now quit calling here. Long distance ain't free and last time I checked, money ain't growing on no trees round here." *Click.*

It would be close to two decades later before I spoke to my mother again. I sat there staring at the phone for about a minute until I finally placed it back in its cradle. I walked to my room and locked the door behind me. I opened my sock drawer and reached for the white pair way in the back. The money was still there. Six hundred and forty dollars even. It felt like a lot until I had to resort to my only other option—buying another house.

My caseworker down at the welfare office had gotten word of what happened and claimed that she'd also received "a number of anonymous tips" that it wasn't the first time that I'd left the kids home alone and that when I was there, I had all types of men coming and going. So, she cut off my food stamps, welfare check— everything.

They may not have known it, but I depended on them girls at that point. I didn't like the sound of that, but it wasn't much else that I could do at the time to change it. What I didn't do, however, is let them know that I depended on them. As much shit that I talked, you would've thought that I had a million dollars saved up in the bank somewhere.

A million dollars wasn't far out of reach either. Not in that line of business, it wasn't. I was a landlady. That carried a nice ring to it: "a landlady." It was like a landlord; landlords manage properties and landladies manage women. Plus, when I think of a landlord, I think of big-bellied white men. A landlady put me in the mind of a fancy woman that wears heels everywhere she goes and has a big, nice house.

I also learned that my house was called a bordello. Bordellos were houses where people went to find prostitutes. I say "people" and not "men" because we've had a woman come through a time or two. Bordellos were one of the first places that men from out of town wanted pointed out. Our first white man to visit the house told me all of this. Funny part was: he wasn't even from New Orleans. He was just so in love with the city that he made it his business to know every nook and cranny of it.

He also said that the city used to have a section marked off just for prostitutes. The authorities wanted to be able to go to one place to check up on them instead of all over town. They claimed that it was strictly for "regulation purposes," but it sounded to me like they wanted to know exactly where to go to get some. President Wilson ordered it to be closed, although the mayor of New Orleans at the time said that it wasn't a good idea. His opinion didn't matter much though. Anybody who watched the news would tell you that federal always trumped state. So, away went Storyville and after it closed, guess what it became? The Iberville Projects—the same place that me, Freckles, and Ann started off at.

Like the church folk say, that was confirmation!

Chapter 9

W hat I forgot to mention was that he also said the police worked in patterns. Prostitution in New Orleans was in full swing during the Storyville days. Then, the authorities cracked down, closed shop, and it seemingly disappeared. The thing was, it never did (and never will). The police just found something else to focus on and whatever they were targeting at the time is what made the front page.

Well the hour hand had once again landed on us. They were picking prostitutes up off of the corners and shutting down bordellos left and right. It wasn't even the local police doing it. It was the National Guard.

I'd stopped letting the girls leave the house and had limited our guests to only the regulars. Until shit cooled off, no new ones were allowed. Once again, Ann's face was balled up like she had a mouthful of ashes. So it shouldn't have surprised me when I walked in one evening to a strange white man sitting on the sofa.

He was clearly drunk out of his mind and rambling. I walked over to take the wobbling glass out of his hand before he spilled liquor all over the place, but ended up spilling it my damn self. He wasn't no strange white man. He was Clarence McPherson, superintendent of the New Orleans Police Department.

I may not have still been lying around on the couch all day, but I still read the paper every morning and watched the news every evening. If he wasn't in the paper, then he was the news. Everybody in New Orleans should've known who he was. I looked over at Freckles and she was looking like my daughter Annette, wearing the look that said that she wasn't to blame; knew who did it, but wouldn't tell. Paulette was too busy laughing after everything he had to say. Ann shrugged and turned up her mouth, letting me know that she'd let him in and was ready to blame me for not being there as her excuse for doing it. I shook my head.

"Mr. McPherson, I think it's time to go. Me and my sisters would like to gone start dinner now," I said politely.

He took his time piercing each of us with his cold, blue eyes. "Sisters? More like whores to me," he said, picking up the glass that I'd knocked over.

"Who he calling a—," Ann started.

I raised my hand to cut her off. "Now ain't no need for name calling Mr. McPherson. We're ladies up in here."

"Like hell. Pour me another drink will you," he said.

Paulette moved toward the kitchen and I stopped her and asked the girls to give me a few minutes with him alone.

"You don' drank it all," I answered him. "Now I know you going through a difficult time right now, but drinking ain't doing nothing but moving the problems around inside of you. It ain't getting rid of 'em."

"How in the hell do you figure I have problem?" he asked.

"I'ma have to ask you to mind your mouth in my house. Like I said, we're ladies here. Now back to what I was saying, I saw what happened down there at the Howard Johnson."

"Were you there?"

"No, it was all over the paper and in the news," I answered.

"So I guess you think I'ma racist too then, huh?"

"I don't know you enough to think nothing about you. All I know is what I see and from what I saw, you didn't do nothing wrong. That man killed seven people. I don't care if he was black or not, wrong is wrong and he deserved what he got."

"So you don't think I made a wrong call?" he asked, looking at me and I could tell that he was really just seeing me as my own woman and not just a black woman.

"Not that time, I don't. Now what happened down there with them Black Panthers is another story."

"They can be just as violent," he said, sticking his chest out. He looked a lot smaller without the uniform on.

"Yeah, but the difference with them is that you got to get violent with them in order for them to get violent with you."

"They involve themselves in affairs that have nothing to do with them!" he yelled. I let it slide.

"It got everything to do with them. Black folk ain't exactly treated like white folk round here."

"And just what in the hell do you mean by that? If you watch the news so much, didn't you see that the Civil Rights Act was just passed?"

"You know very well what I mean," I said.

"Yeah, yeah. Where's my drink? Didn't I ask for a damn drink?"

"I don' told you once already about cussing up in here," I warned.

He smiled. "You know what? I like you. You seem like a real take-no-bull kind of woman. What's your name?"

"Josephine," I lied, choosing my idol's name. I also decided that from then on out, that was what I would go by. Louisa was dead and Josephine had taken her place. Once the girls made the change, that would seal the deal.

"Josephine. You don't look much like a Josephine, but I like it on you."

"Thank you. Now that we've been introduced, if you don't mind…"

"Josephine, do you mind if I stop by every now and then to share a drink or two with you?"

"Now you don' already accused us of being whores. Should I expect to be arrested after having this drink with you?" I asked.

"No, no, no. That's not my fight to fight. You see the National Guard here, don't you? That's because I refuse to let my men get involved. We got bigger issues to deal with in this city like drugs and violence. I happen to love whorehouses myself."

"I hear you talking," I said, walking toward the back door to let him out. No way I could let him out the front and risk my customers seeing that.

"I'll be back next week, same time, for that drink," he said and winked.

"That won't be necessary. Me and you both are already spoken for."

He kissed my hand. "It's a date. See you then gorgeous."

And he came too and kept coming. We never even had sex. We got together, had some drinks, and talked. I would call him on his bullshit and he would call me on mine. He knew that I ran a whorehouse—or a bordello, whatever you want to call it—but I refused to admit it. Something told me that I could trust him, but I chose not to trust that feeling. If I had to go down then so be it, but I wasn't going down like no sucker.

I would ask him about stuff that was in the news and he would give me the real deal on what was going on. He also looked out for my place. When doors started getting kicked in, mine was safe. I would almost get to thinking that we were something like friends, then he would slip and say "nigger," but I didn't get mad. What for? I said "cracker" just as much as they say "nigger." Plus, I was putting in work for black folk. I guess you could say that I was a part of the Civil Rights Movement. Police wasn't getting away with beating up and killing on black men like they used to. That much was for sure.

I enjoyed our time together. It was much different than the time I spent with Conti. Me and Conti talked about the clouds, seem like. We talked about stuff that wasn't never going to happen, like us getting married, having more kids, and moving back to Africa. Me and McPherson talked about real life stuff, stuff that mattered and made a difference. I didn't even charge him for our times together and I didn't have to. He spent so much money on me that you would've thought that I was his wife and not that scarecrow looking thing that graced the news with him every now and then.

He took me to fancy restaurants and trips out of town where we stayed in fancy hotels. He bought me furs and even hired me some help—from a white lady. Can you imagine that? She showed up and I turned her right back around. That's the last kind of trouble that I needed. He bought me a car and paid my house off for me. He said that *"as long as you were making payments, then it wasn't yours."* I made sure that every bill, title, and receipt had my name on it. Earl taught me that.

That was good timing for me. Once the house was paid off, that gave me money and credit to get another house. Since the new house was in a much better neighborhood, I put the kids there. That helped me to sleep a little better at night. They had a little more room, a grocery store right up the street, furniture, food, and they were far enough away from the other house that I didn't have to worry about any of them popping up.

McPherson seemed like the perfect fit for my life at the time. I dare not say forever because circumstances would have never allowed that. Plus, I was smart enough to know that nothing lasted forever.

Sure enough, it started getting…uncomfortable. The FBI was busting politicians, judges, and police on charges of corruption. When I first started asking McPherson about it, he would wave it off. Then, he got to acting all nervous. He was always drunk and had even started smoking. When I asked him about it, he said that he used to smoke but had stopped.

"What made you start back?" I asked.

"Leave it alone," his mouth said and his eyes begged me not to probe.

I left it alone. I didn't ask another question, but after I read that he was under investigation, I decided to cut it off. It was getting too dangerous, too fast. The best way to do it was to get straight to the point and leave right afterwards. I should've learned, by then, that nothing happened the way that I intended.

I met him in his office one Wednesday evening. It was after hours and I knew that he would be the only one there. He was looking out of the window and his back was to the door. He heard and saw everything, so I knew that he had heard the door open. Yet, he never bothered to turn around. He just stood in front of the window overlooking the city with his hands in his pockets. Uniform starched to a crisp. They could stand alone had he not been wearing them. I cleared my throat, readying myself for my announcement. I closed the door softly behind me, but didn't bother to lock it. I would say what I had to say and turn and walk away. Simple as that.

"We can't keep doing this."

He didn't respond. He didn't move. If I didn't know him any better, I would say that he didn't even hear me.

"Did you hear me?" I asked him in a raised tone.

Still, nothing. I walked over to him to demand a response and that's when I noticed the tears in his eyes. I peered out of the window, trying to locate the catalyst of his stirred emotions, but all

I saw was downtown New Orleans: people coming and going, selling and buying, but nothing unusual. I looked at him again, his gaze unmoved. I stood next to him. I couldn't leave at that point, because he had invited me into his world of hurt. We stood there looking out on the city for a cold, hard minute until he finally broke.

"This wasn't the city I was raised in."

I could tell that this was about to be another *nonversation*, so I just let him talk.

"I was raised in a decent city. A catholic city. It wasn't perfect, but hell, what city is perfect? A few bad seeds planted in my soil," he said through clenched teeth, "and sprouted more gambling, killing, corruption, and drugs than one can bear."

He lowered himself onto the edge of the desk. His shoulders were slumped and his back was rounded. I'd never seen him so...low. It made him look ten years older.

"Before I knew how to clean my own ass, I knew I wanted to be a cop." He chuckled under his breath the way crazy folk do before losing it. "My daddy was the superintendent at the time I entered the force. He warned me not to fool with it, wanting me to go to college, be a lawyer, and then a judge. That's not what I wanted for myself though, so I jumped in." He mimicked his father's voice. "'New Orleans police cut from a small cloth son. You made outta dat kinda fabric?'" He continued, "I said, 'yes sir.' He said, 'Well hand me ya' soul and take dis here badge.' I laughed, but I'll be damned if it ain't what I don' up and done."

Then he lost it. He started bawling right there at his desk. He got to confessing sins that he'd committed as a police trying to climb the ladder and the ones that he made as the superintendent trying to maintain his position. I stood in front of him and he wrapped his arms around my waist. It was then that I could smell the liquor on him. I didn't judge him for it though. The man was already down and out. I just rubbed his back in the way that only a mother could do.

He buried his face in my chest and released hard, heavy sobs. I didn't know what to say and silence felt too awkward so I started to hum. We stayed like that for a whole song and eventually the tears stopped. His hands slid past my waist, over my hips, and down my thighs. He came back up, going beneath my dress. He gripped my behind with both of his hands and squeezed like he knew that it would be the last time that he would ever see me again. His lips found my breasts, my neck, ears, cheek, and mouth.

The tobacco was disgusting, but the passion was like nothing I'd ever tasted before. It slipped past our lips all the way down to my toes, setting fire to my feet. I climbed onto his lap while he unbuttoned my dress. I kissed the top of his head, neverminding the sweat as he busied himself in my bosom. We were seconds away from going there when the door opened. We both jumped up and the last person in the world that expected to see walked in.

Conti.

"I knew it! I knew it!" he yelled. "I followed you. I wanted to make you my wife. Is this what I deserve? For the white man?"

Tears streamed down his face as he was pointed at us. Before I could stop him, he charged at McPherson like a bull that saw red. He sent McPherson flying back onto the window. He grabbed McPherson's stiff, starched collar and bared his bottom teeth like he was ready to kill. The veins in his neck bulged like the muscles in his back.

"You know you don' messed up don't you, boy?" McPherson asked. The way he said "boy" made the hairs on my arms stand at attention.

McPherson reached for his gun and I turned to leave. I refused to witness what was about to happen. I opened the door and was met face to face with a uniformed officer. He held an open folder and dropped it when he saw me. He looked me up and down and then peeked into the office.

"Oh shit," he muttered. He reached for his gun, ran into the room, and pressed the black barrel into the back of Conti's head.

"Please, no," I begged. "God, no. Please."

Conti raised his hands above his head. His nose was still a hair away from McPherson's face. They stared each other down like a bell would ring at any moment. McPherson smiled and ordered the officer to take him away. The officer knocked him upside the head with the gun, causing him to fall to the ground. On his way down, McPherson kneed him in the face. The other officer stepped onto Conti's back with his black, heavy boot and clanked a pair of shiny metal cuffs onto his wrists.

As Conti was being escorted out of the room, he stared at me through his one good eye. The other eye had already swollen shut. I wanted to cry for him, but I knew that it would do no good. I counted to thirty to give them enough time to get down the hall before making my own exit. I touched the door knob and was choked by my own dress, drug backwards, and slammed up against the wall.

Now McPherson's blood-red face was pressed against mine and he looked like he wanted to kill me. For a second, I thought that he would. My heartbeat was beginning to pound in my ears and I knew from my fights with Walter that it would only be a matter of seconds before I passed out. He let me go and my feet dropped to the floor and I stumbled. While dangling in midair, they had fallen asleep. He kicked me and I covered my face.

"Do you know how much hell I'm going through? Do you think I'm about to let some coon bitch and her nigger put the nail in my coffin? Huh? Do you?!"

I didn't answer.

"Get up!" he ordered.

I didn't move.

He grabbed me by the back of my dress and pulled me to my feet as if I were nothing but a two- pound raggedy Ann doll. I could hear my dress splitting and see that the front was stained with blood. I could taste it; a lot of it, so I knew that it was coming from my mouth. I ran my tongue across the top and bottom rows to makes sure that all of my teeth were still there. They were.

"Now get out," he said.

I turned to leave. I couldn't speak if I wanted to because I had a mouthful of blood. Once in the hall, I spat it out on the wall. It didn't make me feel better though. I still felt like shit. No, I felt worse than shit. I couldn't face the girls like that so I went home to my kids instead. I hadn't seen them in months, so when I walked in the front door, all of them except for 'Nette stood there looking crazy.

The laughter that I'd heard coming from house while walking up the road had ceased along with the aromas from the stove and even the music had somehow found its way to the end of the last song.

Doris moseyed from the back of the house holding two albums asking why the party had stopped. She saw me and stopped dead in her tracks. It was like I was looking at my daughter for the first time in years instead of months. She was the same height as me, had the breasts and hips of a woman, and was wearing a pair of my heels.

After a stare down that lasted for a spell, she dropped the albums that she was holding and stormed out of the house, brushing shoulders with me. One of the boys ran after her. I didn't try to stop her. Hell, I didn't even turn around. I was too tired. I told the other two boys to leave. Mona stood there staring at me like she had something to say, but didn't know how to say it.

"Instead of standing there looking stupid, you could be getting this house in order," I told her.

Annette clung to my legs, pressing on what had to be bruises because it hurt like hell. I told her to go run me some bathwater. She took off down the hall.

Doris had moved all of her shit in my room. I picked it all up and in one heap and dropped all of it on the floor in the bedroom directly across from mine—the room that the first three shared.

Reta was on her knees folding clothes like she ain't had shit to do with shit when I told her to come and unfasten my shoes. It hurt enough to move, let alone bending over. She did as she was told, no questions asked.

"I thought you said that you were going to the store to buy some milk and would be right back," Reta said as respectfully as she could.

She was old enough to know what she was doing. She figured that if she asked with a soft enough voice that she could avoid getting smacked in the damn mouth which is exactly what I would've done if I weren't in so much pain. Annette ran in the room, announcing that the bathwater was ready.

"Thank you, baby. Now go fix Mama something to drank."

She skipped away to do as I asked her to do. She knew exactly how to fix my drink. She knew that water was water and that a coke was a coke, but a "drank" was the stuff in the Mason jar from the back of the cabinet behind the seasonings that look like water but taste like fire. It was the only drink that was poured into the one crystal glass in the house.

"Huh, Mama?" Reta asked.

"Just 'cause you got some little nigga running round thinking you cute, don't think that give you the right to be questioning me. Now mind your damn mouth before you end up getting slapped in it."

"Yes, ma'am," she answered with her eyes to the floor. She walked out as Nette was walking back in the room with my drank.

I finished the cup in one swallow, pressed my chest until the burning stopped, and then handed Nette the cup back.

"And close the door behind you. I need a nap," I said.

"Yes, ma'am."

Chapter 10

"You gotta hold your head up too, Reta."

"Doris, I know. Leave me alone and go back to bed."

"I'm not either because you'll drip it everywhere and I'll have to clean that shit up."

"Stop fucking cursing at me!"

I slowly woke up from the deep sleep that I'd been drowning in. I was so deep into the sleep that I was dreaming in my dream. Moonshine will do that to you. My hearing was the last of my five senses to wake up, finally realizing that somebody was arguing.

"Well if you quit acting like a child then maybe I will stop fucking cursing at you. Now hold your head back and pinch right here."

It had to be Doris and Reta.

"What y'all doing in there?" I yelled from my bed.

"My nose bleeding and I'm trying to tell Doris that I got it, but she won't leave me alone and she making it worse."

"I am not. I know what I'm doing. Mona! Mona, come here!" Doris yelled.

"Get your damn hands out of my face!" Reta snapped at Doris.

I climbed out of bed to see what the hell was going on and to shut it down so that I could get back to sleep. The window units, which weren't worth a damn, were frozen over again so the house was hot as hell. I never would've realized it had they not waken me up. Only another drink was going to get me back to sleep in that heat.

"Dammit Mona, don't you hear me calling you, girl?" Doris hollered.

"I don't know who told y'all that it was okay to cuss in my house, but until you get your own shit, you better watch your mouth and I mean that."

Doris rolled her eyes and stormed out of the bathroom. I turned around and yanked her back so fast that I didn't even notice that I'd grabbed the child's hair and not her shirt.

"Let me go!"

"Little girl, you are a child and a child ain't no match for a woman. Remember that," I said through my teeth.

"From what I heard, women raise children. Now if you'll excuse me, I gotta child with a bloody nose and a child that ain't answering me that I gotta tend to right now."

I let her go. She marched to the room that she shared with the twins and started cussing up a storm. I ran to the room ready to check her until I saw that Mona was down on the floor on her hands and knees. Her back was rounded and she was breathing like she'd just finished getting the behind whooping of her life.

Then I remembered. She had asthma. Doris rubbed her back, reminding her to calm down and to breathe in through her nose and out through her mouth. She barked off some more orders and like the perfect little soldiers, everybody did their part. Nette brought the inhaler from the kitchen and Doris coaxed Mona through the whole process. Pam cleaned up the mess that Doris sure enough said that Reta would make. I stood there looking and feeling out of place and in the way. They carried on as if I weren't even there and before the hour was over, they were all back in the bed like nothing had even happened.

I woke up the next morning feeling even more out of place and in the way. I felt useless and damn near invisible. The only ones that acknowledged me were Nette and Pam and even then, it was only when they wanted something. Before I could move to get to it, Doris would have already gotten it and moved on to the next thing. She thought she was so damn grown. For one, she walked too damn fast for my taste. She didn't know how to talk to nobody and her face was always twisted up like somebody owed her something.

"Ain't you supposed to be at school?" I asked her one morning.

She stopped cutting the chicken to look up at me. "Are you serious?"

"Do I look like I'm playing? I ain't raising no dummies."

"You ain't raising nobody," she mumbled under her breath, thinking that I didn't hear her.

"What did you just say, little girl?" I asked.

She sighed like she'd just finished an eight-hour shift and put her fist on her hip. "I was going to school up until two months ago. I didn't stop going by choice. As a matter of fact, I liked school. I was making real good grades and a few of my teachers had even told me that they would help me apply for college."

"Something about that don't sit right with me. Sounds to me that if you were college material then you would be at school and not in the kitchen playing with chicken."

"I'm playing with chicken so that my sisters will have something to eat when they get home. If you were here then you would know that. And I dropped out of school because no matter how hard I tried, it just wasn't enough hours in the day to try to be a straight-A student and a mama of four kids." Her bottom lip began to tremble and tears shot down her face.

I wanted to reach out to her, but I knew that she wouldn't come to me. I could never be a mother to her again. It dawned on me. That's why she felt that she could cuss in my presence, roll her eyes at me, and ignore me. There was no respect there—no boundaries, no love, and no hope. There was too much distance, too much time, and too many misunderstandings standing between us.

It was no wonder that I had been feeling out of place. *I was in the way.* There was no way that I could do for the girls what she'd been doing. When I walked in the room and saw Mona bent over, I froze up. It took me time to remember that the girl had asthma. That was enough time for her to have died. I didn't know that Pam liked a spoon of sugar in her oatmeal and that Nette only liked socks that came up to her knees and that Mona had to use Dreft detergent and that Reta was lactose intolerant. Hell, I didn't even know what lactose intolerant was until Nette told me.

I might have carried all five of them and pushed them all out, but I wasn't a mother to them. God must have forgotten to turn my mama button on, because the only emotion that ever surfaced was anger. I could not think of one happy memory as a mother. Come to think of it, I probably wasn't even meant to be a mama.

I belonged on the other side of town and in another world— the world that was tucked up under this one—the one that rebels found first, church folk pointed fingers at, and hypocrites couldn't leave alone. Don't get me wrong now. There were problems down there too, but those were a different kind of problems. Emotions didn't have a place in them kind of problems so I was better equipped to handle them.

I took a nice slow bath, hoping that all my thoughts would go down the drain along with the water when it came time to get out. They didn't. The kids had gotten out of school and came running in the house, talking over each other about their day. Doris already had dinner cooked. Nette came to ask me if I wanted to eat with them, but I politely said no. She walked out and I went back to getting dressed.

I wrote a note to Doris telling her that I had to leave, but would send enough money every week to help take care of things. I put it in the drawer where she kept her underwear and took one last look in the mirror. I smiled, satisfied that I was doing the right thing and proud that I had the courage to do it.

"I'll be back," I said casually, walking past the kitchen.

"Where you going, Mama?" Nette asked.

"To the store," I answered.

"You coming back?" Annette had asked the question, but the way that Doris looked me said that she was the one waiting on the answer.

"Yeah, I'm coming back."

"What you going to get?" Annette asked, full of questions.

"Some cigarettes," I lied.

"I didn't know you smoked," Doris said with her mouth twisted up and her arms folded across her chest.

"I just started," I answered and made my way on out the door, letting the door slam shut behind me.

I climbed in my burgundy Cutlass Supreme and pulled off. As much as I loved my car, I had to sell it and find something else. McPherson bought it for me and now that he'd shown me his ugly side, I didn't want or need any more shit. Although the car was in my name, he had three upper hands on me: a dick, white skin, and a badge.

I pulled up to the house and when I opened the front door, I started coughing and my eyes started burning. Sticks of incense burned from big, fake plants that someone thought looked good. I trashed all of it and then opened the windows to air the house out. I heard giggling and music coming from the back which told me that I wasn't there alone.

I'd warned the girls more than once about them all being locked up in bedrooms. It was important on so many levels for someone to be up front. The police could show up, we could be robbed, or anything. I decided to wait until they came out to talk to them about it. At that moment, I needed a nap. I'd had a hell of a day. Little did I know…it was just getting started.

The door to my bedroom, which was where the music and giggles were coming from, was locked. I knocked like a madwoman and damn near kicked the door in, waiting for whoever the hell was in my space to open the damn door. Ann peeked her head out with a big, goofy grin on her face. I pushed the door open, throwing her back. She had some nappy head sucker laid up in my bed wearing nothing but draws and socks. She had moved the record player from up front to my bedroom and it wasn't until I caught the whiff of reefer that I really lost it.

"Have you lost your mind?!"

"No, but you clearly must have," she answered.

"I am going to count to ten and I swear before God, both of y'all better be out of my house."

"I ain't going nowhere," she said and then folded her arms across her chest.

Somebody should've told her what I'd been going through with Doris. I'd just handed one set of reigns over and I'd be damn if I was giving up my last set. Somebody should've told her that I was hungry, my head was hurting, and I was dead tired. Maybe then, she wouldn't have come at me like that.

But she did.

I slapped the hell out of her. Everything, for a second, went completely silent. Before she had time to come around, I popped her again and pushed her into the corner behind the door. She tried to fight back, but she didn't have room to do much of nothing. After getting her head banged into the wall enough times, she finally crouched down and shielded her head with her arms. I started stomping her then—right on the top of her head. I don't know who she *thought* I was. Did she expect me to bow down, apologize, and go sleep in the front room? In my house?

Freckles and Paulette had to peel me off of her and I still didn't stop. I took my shoe off and shot it clean across the room. It missed her barely. She called me everything but a child of God, but what she wasn't doing was standing around with her arms crossed anymore. She was packing her bags so fast you would've thought that I shot a bullet instead of a shoe. Her little friend had dressed, eased past us, and was gone before I could get to him next.

After Ann left, I put my foot down. I'd never done it right the first time around. Rules popped up as stuff went down, but not this time. I gave it to them flat out:

Someone is to be up front at all times.

If I have never seen him before, then he is not to be in this house.

Half of whatever is made belongs to me. Lying is cheating and cheating is stealing and I don't play too nice with thieves.

Clean up behind yourselves.

If someone is giving you a problem, let me know. Don't wait until somebody is trying to kick my damn door down to tell me.

If you think you caught something, you did. Take a few days off and get it taken care of.

My bedroom is off limits every second of every day. Trespassers will be shot.

"If you got a problem with any of that, then you are free to leave now," I said, still breathing hard.

Neither of them had anything to say. I preferred it that way. I dismissed Paulette, but kept Freckles around for a bit. She caught me up with what I'd missed while gone. Madam Young, from around the corner, had been raided, but they didn't find nothing. A few strange white men had come knocking at the door, but they turned each of them away, fearing that they were cops. I nodded.

"Since y'all were still working while I was gone, then I should have some money, right?"

She shrugged. "Ann got it. She said that since—"

I raised my hand to stop her. My blood pressure was rising again. I could feel it. My headache was getting so bad that it was starting to mess with my vision. I couldn't take any more for one day so I walked off to make sure that my sock money was still there—it was. Next, I fixed myself a drank and got in the bed—after I changed my sheets.

I dreamt that I woke up to a room full of gold. The sun positioned itself right in front of my window and the gold began to melt. My room began to flood and the door moved further and further away. The sun took on the face of my beloved grandmother, but instead of helping me, she shook her head as if disappointed.

The dreams got even crazier as time went on. Another night, I had a dream that I was walking down a busy, overly crowded street. I knew every single person on the street. Some were from Coushatta and others from New Orleans. None of them recognized me however, and when I tried to reach out to them, it was as if they couldn't hear me or feel me grab them.

I was a firm believer that all dreams carried meaning and I was anxious to know what mine meant. So, I made a trip to Bayou Teche to see about, what many called, the devil's work. Women went there to get rid of their pregnancies; men went there to get rid of their wives; the sick went there for healing after losing hope that religion would get the job done; and there were those like me, who went for some interpretation and a peek into the future.

Chapter 11

T *he bullfrogs sing when rain is coming.* It took me over two
hours and a full tank of gas to make that trip to Bayou
Teche. Then, when I get there, I paid her twenty dollars and
all she had to tell me was about some damn bullfrogs. I let that sit
at the front of my mind for weeks, but I didn't hear a thing. In fact,
I had no complaints. I was making money again and plenty of it. I
went to bed one night thinking about how we needed more girls—
at least three. The next day, two showed up at the front door: Mary
and Rose, the twins from down at the club. They said that the
Black Cat had been taken over, renamed, and Burlesque wasn't in
the plans.

A few weeks later, a white girl showed up. I didn't trust her
and just knew that she was what we called "a plant." Paulette
swore by her and after much debating, I finally agreed to give her
a chance. Her name was Jacquelyn. She had long, brown hair that
hung to the middle of her back. A tattoo ran from her right ankle
up past her skirt line. She wore red lipstick, red fingernail polish,
and smoked cigars. I told her that smoking wasn't allowed in my
house and she shot back that she had her own house.

"Then why do you need to work here?" I asked.

"For clients. I'm new in town. Plus, bordellos tend to be
safer."

"I guess you want to work from 9 to 5 too," I said.

"Yes, please. Well, nine at night until five in the morning, that is. I would like to be home in time to watch Love of Life and Get Christie Love!"

I looked her over real good. "Most of our customers are black. We get some white ones too, but they're black mainly. The customers get to make the choice though."

"I don't see black or white. I only see beauty or the lack thereof."

I was really looking at her crazy then. I crossed my arms over my chest and leaned against the door. "And just where are you from?"

"Paris," she answered. "But I moved to Canada as a girl, studied in London, and married in Italy. He was your typical Italian man, which isn't so much a bad thing. It's just not exactly a good thing for the type of girl like me. I'm more of a Mistinguett, Marilyn Monroe, or Josephine Baker type of girl, which probably has much to do with my upbringing. My mother, too, is from Paris. She paints for a living. My father, a writer, happens to be from South Africa. So, I guess that makes me more Afro-American than you," she joked.

That was just our first conversation. That girl would talk you into a dream and back. We couldn't wait until morning came and she left. Well, all of us but Paulette. She ate the stories up like fresh peach cobbler with a side of vanilla ice cream. She couldn't get enough, but I'd had enough. You couldn't mention a place outside of New Orleans without her throwing her two cents in. According to her, she's been all over the world and met every famous person that you can think of.

I went ahead and asked her once, "Well if you know so much and been every damn where, why you gotta do what you do for the next dollar?"

She smiled. "It's another story to add to the book that I'll one day write." She threw her head back and laughed.

Paulette stared at her, unaware of the smile that was spread across her own face. The poor child was like one of those fish that sucked on the glass of the fish tank. Jacquelyn couldn't go to the toilet without Paulette waiting outside the door. She'd even picked up Jacquelyn's accent a little bit, sounding like a damn fool.

I didn't mess with her about it, because it was making me money. Jacquelyn had a way of only messing with one or two men at a time. When I say "at a time," I mean months. They paid so much money that no one could complain. See, one thing that I never did with my girls was to tell them who to lay down with. That wasn't for me to do, but Jacquelyn taught me something—even if she didn't mean to. I was losing a lot of money by giving the girls so much freedom.

The problem was that I felt that they were doing me a favor. In actuality, it was the other way around. That mentality gave me a little more backbone. Instead of telling them who to lay with, I told them how much money to turn in every month. If they didn't have it, then they would be cut loose. That gave them the option to up their prices or "put in more work."

Jacquelyn ended up schooling Freckles and Paulette. Mary had too much pride to be taught anything by anybody. She was another one that wanted to believe that she had shit all figured out. Her poor sister, Rose, didn't want to start no conflict with her sister so she followed behind everything she did.

Before you knew it, Freckles, Jacquelyn, and Paulette were pulling in heavy weight for some light work while the twins worked their back loose in the name of pride. Out of all of them, I still made more off of Jacquelyn. She didn't live in the house; she was just using me for my safety net, so I had to charge her extra for that. Why she never went to one of the houses down the street? I'll never know because I never bothered to ask.

Then one morning, she came to me looking all pale in the face. She needed a favor, a big one. I thought it was going to be

128

about money and my mouth got to twitching. That's how fast I was ready to say no. That's not what she came for though. She wanted to move in. One of her johns had broken into her house and was waiting, in her bed, for her one morning. She got him out with no trouble, but it scared her too badly to stay. She even offered to pay more, but I told her to just keep the fee where it was. I wouldn't accept the increase because greed would bite you in the ass, I also didn't lower it because the risk of having a white girl in my house was too costly.

We had plenty of customers, which meant plenty of money, plenty of food, and plenty good times. What we didn't have was space. Once upon a time, the three-bedroom house was a godsend. Jacquelyn and the twins ran the number of occupants up to six. Without Conti, McPherson, or the kids, it wasn't many moments that I wasn't there. We were really packed in there like sardines. Our cycles got to be on the same exact schedule, so when the third week of the month rolled around, we were some fussing, feisty fishes.

That was our week to hang our "Gone on Vacation" sign on the front door, go shopping, eating, dancing, and whatever else it was that we wanted to do. We rarely went out together. In fact, I preferred to go out alone. It gave me time to think, clear my head, and plan the next move. That's exactly what I was coming home from doing when I saw Paulette's head sticking out of the door, talking to a random white man on the porch.

I walked up and spoke. He turned around, smiled, and extended his hand for me to shake it. I looked it at, but never offered him mine in return. He looked familiar—dangerously familiar. Blonde hair, blue eyes, short in height, thin in build, and wore a shiny blue class ring. Class ring. Class. Then it hit me. He was one of the recent graduates of the police academy that I'd seen in the paper not too long ago.

I made it my business to study their faces. I would even quiz myself by covering up their names and try to put a face to the name. I didn't know when the day would come or how the situation would present itself, but I knew that the information would come in handy. I couldn't remember this little fella's name, but definitely his face.

"How can I help you?" I asked, interrupting the introduction that Paulette was giving.

"I was just stopping by for dinner, ma'am. I heard that you all were having a pot of spaghetti tonight," he said, referencing our customer's secret code. I made a mental note to change it ASAP.

"We weren't expecting company. You see, we not—"

"I can handle it, Josephine. I'm sure," Paulette cut in, giving me the big eyes. "It shouldn't be much to put on a pot of spaghetti," she added.

"That won't be necessary," I said to her, frowning. I turned my attention back to him. "As I was saying, we ain't from 'round here and ain't much accustomed to having guests. Now, may I ask who sent you?"

"A good friend to us both," He answered.

"And who is this good friend?"

He opened his mouth then closed it right back. He did that twice, scratched the back of his head, and said, "He begged me not to share that information."

"Is that right?" I said, dramatically placing my hand over my chest. "He doesn't sound much like a good friend at all."

He took a deep breath, looked around, and leaned in toward me. "I don't want any trouble, ma'am. I'm just looking for a good time. Like you, I'm new in town. I have two hundred dollars in my wallet and I'm looking to spend it all right now."

I put a hand on his shoulder. "We're blessed already, but I thank you for the offer. I'm sure that the church down there could make good use of it."

"I have to be to work in about two hours and I need to spend this money soon. Know what I mean?"

"What you do for a living to be offering that kind of money? A man, such as yourself, with good looks and money should be married with kids by now."

His ears turned red. He must have felt it because he reached up and scratched one then shoved his hands into front pockets. "Well should I come back at a better time?"

"Not really, no. We're actually very private and would prefer to keep it that way," I said, walking into the house.

"You'll regret this," he mumbled, jogging down the porch steps.

I rolled my eyes and went in the house, priding myself on dodging such a close call and laughing at McPherson for thinking that he could fool me with an amateur. His putting his hands on me wasn't enough. It was then obvious that he wanted to bring me down. The federal government had been pressuring local governments to take action, threatening to stop grants and whatnot if they refused. I got that, I watched the news. That didn't mean that I had to be targeted. He had the say on which houses went down and during our time together, he made it his business to keep mine safe.

Needless to say, that time was over and two mornings later, my door got kicked in. Luckily, we had no customers. Six uniformed officers raided the place like we were numbers 1-6 on America's Most Wanted. They kicked bedroom doors open that could have easily been opened with a simple twist of the knob, flipped furniture over, tore clothes off hangers, and checked every corner that a roach could hide in.

They busted us for words on a piece of paper. Freckles had been keeping a diary and in it, she mentioned random happenings in the house. Naturally, the "business transactions" were included. They confiscated my money, jewels, and everything else of value, claiming that it was evidence. Evidence my ass. I spent a whole four days in jail. Since they had my money, I couldn't bail myself out or hire an attorney.

They separated the six of us which meant that they had to keep us in our own little rooms which consisted of four grey walls and barely enough room for a cot and a pisser. I wrote a letter to Doris explaining that the money would be a little late that week. In truth, I only hoped that it was a little late. I'd prepped my nerves to handle a week. Anything longer and I was going to lose my damn mind and land myself some serious time.

I felt like the one gorilla in the zoo. Guards would stop by just to see who I was and some had the nerve to ask me if everything they'd been hearing about me was true. One had even brought his brother just to shake my hand. Sometimes, it was okay. It threw a little glitter on my jumpsuit learning that I was some kind of local celebrity. Other times I would dare one more person to come peeking inside my cell. Luckily for them and me, they wouldn't come unless it was to bring me food or haul me down to the shower.

On the third day, I got a letter from an unknown author with no return address. It was written on fancy paper and with an equally fancy pen—the kind that you have to dip in ink. It definitely wasn't a love letter though. The handwriting was a woman's. The g's, p's, and y's looped real pretty like. But the tone was a man's. There were four straight-to-the-point sentences lined up like a poem:

Your whores are your commodity.

Keep both eyes open.

Never smile at a john.

Know your rights.

The next day, we were bailed out and I was met by a lawyer that introduced herself as Charlotte Brown, named after the first female black lawyer. Her hair was pulled up into a tight bun. She wore little makeup, lipstick that needed to be touched up, a business skirt with the matching jacket, decent stockings, and a low heel.

I asked her when I would go to court. She said that it wasn't necessary; she had already taken care of everything. My fourth amendment right had been violated. I asked her what exactly my fourth amendment right was. She handed me two sheets of paper stapled together. The top of it read: Bill of Rights.

"Well that sounds like a lawsuit to me," I said, raising my voice.

"Don't push it." Her tone was much lower, almost a whisper. She handed me a thick manila folder.

"These are the local and state laws. I would suggest that you familiarize yourself with them. Bear in mind that they can change at any time. I would also suggest that you consider hiring an attorney—someone that understands your line of business." She paused for a moment before continuing. "Jail is the worse place and time to begin looking for an attorney."

"So are you my attorney now?" I asked.

"Should you decide that, then my contact information is written on the inside of the folder," she said, pointing to the bundle in my hands.

"How much for all of this?" I asked, digging into the bag of my returned belongings.

She held up her hand. "This go round was sponsored."

"By who?" I asked.

She smiled and I noticed that she was actually pretty and kind of young. "I'm not at liberty to discuss."

Three weeks later on December 14, 1974 she called me down to her office to go over everything that she was once "not at liberty to discuss." The person that had written me the letter and hired Charlotte for me was the same person. It was a woman, a white woman. In the words of Charlotte, she was a lot like me. She was Ms. Norma Wallace—one of New Orleans' wealthiest, respected, loved, and hated. She took no shit from no one and lived a life that was worth reading in a book or seeing on film.

"How did she die?" I asked, remembering seeing her on television not long ago.

"A single gunshot wound. Self-inflicted."

"What? Why?" I asked.

"Well, anyone that knows Norma knows that she was known to lie about her real age. She vowed to never get old."

"I'm sorry to hear that. I'm sure her kids are taking it the worse. I'll be sure to keep them in my prayers," I said, grabbing my purse.

"She had no kids. That's why you're here today. She willed you her house."

"Excuse me?"

"In her will, she explicitly expressed that you were to have her residence located at 1026 Conti Street. If, by chance, you died before her or refused to take it, then it is to be donated."

"She didn't even know me," I whispered.

Charlotte shrugged. "She liked you. She wasn't a mother, but...are you a mother?" she asked.

I paused. "No," I answered, shaking my head.

"Well mothers tend to have those second pair of eyes. I know my mother did. She could hear and see everything. That's how Norma was. She knew everything about everybody, especially her competition. In her words, you were different from the others. She could see her reflection in you."

"I don't know what to say," I said.

She opened a box, a regular cardboard box, and pulled out two books. They looked like bibles, only smaller. Both of them were black, but one was bigger than the other. There were no words on the cover, but the insides were loaded with them. I was sure of that because I could smell the decades on them.

"She also wanted you to have these. Read them carefully. And if you have no other questions, then I need to you to sign and date on each of the highlighted lines. It's to my understanding that you go by the name of Josephine. However, in your best interest, please use your legal name." She handed me a pen.

I reached in my purse and retrieved my own. I signed my chosen legal name, Josephine, everywhere that I was asked to, shook her hand, grabbed my new belongings, and made my way back to the house to let the girls know the good news. We no longer had to be bunched or reminded of the raid at every turn. We got a new place.

The way the girls were acting would've had you believe that it was Christmas time in the orphanage. They went so far as to put their heads and wallets together to buy me gifts. Freckles bought me a black book, claiming that every madam was supposed to have one. I joked that she must not have learned her lesson about keeping notes. Paulette bought me a bottle of rose water. The twins got me a robe, but I'm sure that it was more of Rose's doing than Mary's. Jacquelyn gave me a shoebox full of red lipstick and red fingernail polish.

"Please don't tell me these are used," I said, chuckling.

"They're all new. I threw mine away. Red is a symbol for passion, power, courage, energy, fire, and desire. Plus, it's sexy. You stand for all of these things. You provide for us a safe space to coexist and I'm sure that it's no easy task. So, this is my way of showing my appreciation."

"Well thank you, Jacquelyn. And what's this here?" I asked, holding up another small, decorated box. The front read: A. Flores.

"Open it and see," she said, smiling.

I opened it and there were neatly stacked brown cigars. They smelled expensive, but I dared not ask how much they cost nor where she got them from. I held the box out to her.

"You know I don't smoke."

"You don't have to. You can just chew on them or keep them for good times' sake. They're also a symbol of power, and wealth too."

So that's how we celebrated our first night in the house. We smoked cigars and drank champagne. Freckles made seafood gumbo that was to die for, and the twins put on a homemade burlesque show. They played Siamese twins. Mary was the naughty one and Rose was the good girl. Jacquelyn and Paulette pretended to be the men in the story. They would keep fighting about it until they finally reached a compromise—they would be good girls one weekend and bad girls the next. That way both girls got their way. The End.

That was about the only time that you saw Mary smile. While on stage, she was in her element. That was her zone and was where she needed to be. That moment paid me my million dollar idea. Not only would we be a house of pretty girls and good loving, but we would have good food, good drinks, and good times. We would put on shows and entertain. The night cap made for customers that couldn't get enough.

Chapter 12

I was busy. Business was booming. Our regular customers had been added to a good chunk of Norma's black book. Thanks to her, we had celebrities. Real celebrities, too: singers, actors (and actresses), and politicians. The governor was a regular. Sometimes he would get so drunk, that he'd go spilling his beans all over the place. He had a wife around the corner, another family across the river, and accepted thousands of dollars' worth of bribes to take care of all of them. I made sure that he went home to his wife a happy man the night he told me that. When he came back, his price had doubled.

He was one of many. In fact, we had more dicks showing up at the door than we could handle. Get this: my best way of managing them was to keep upping my price. They paid it too and on New Year's Eve, not only did I celebrate 1977. I also celebrated being a millionaire. I'd outnumbered Norma and finally hired the accountant that she'd suggested in her books of advice. Next to his name, title, and phone number, she'd written:

He knows business. Know what I mean?

Had it not been for Norma's books, I would have lost my mind. She taught me how to count my money and where to keep it. I never thought the day would come, but it did. She also let me know that it was okay to keep my money in the bank, but to make sure that I paid my taxes on it. I didn't trust it much, so I would put half in and keep half out.

I came to learn that the more I made, then the less that I got to trust anyone or anything. I met a few men, but I never let them get too close. I felt like they only wanted me for my money or my name and I couldn't afford to lose either. Norma swore by younger men who knew nothing and had nothing. That wasn't my thing. They did nothing for me. One tried to hold my attention, but I couldn't stop thinking that I had stretch marks older than him. What could he possibly do for me?

A man was what I needed. I couldn't really enjoy myself for fear of getting pregnant. Rose had gotten pregnant and decided not to keep it. The surgery kept her down for almost two weeks. The poor child looked worse than I did after 13 hours of labor with Pam. The next day, Mary brought a pack of birth control pills home for everybody. I took my first one and thought about what a difference it could've made in my life had the pills been available to me when I was younger.

The thought made me think of my girls. Come to find out, Freckles had been going over to see them without my knowing. I didn't mind though. To be honest, I couldn't have been any more grateful. I was getting suspicious of the mail man stealing the money that I was asking him to deliver to them. I asked Freckles if she would take the money with her on her trips to see them. She didn't mind at all. In turn, I treated her to a little lagniappe.

I choked on my water the day that Freckles came back and told me that Doris was gone. She'd met some white man, called herself falling in love, and picked up and left. Just like that. Just up and left her sisters to fend for themselves. Freckles said not to worry about it and that's what I focused on not doing—worrying. Supposedly Mona had picked up where Doris left off at. That was a little soothing because I knew that Mona had a good head on her shoulders. I told myself that I wasn't worried. My mouth never spoke it, but my body showed it. I went from chewing the cigars to actually smoking them.

Not even a whole year later, she reported back to me that Reta was pregnant. I fell out of my damn chair. I didn't know what to do. I called, Annette picked up, and I hung the phone back up. I felt like calling was a coward move. So, I got dressed and drove down there. I made it up the driveway, up the porch steps, and raised my fist to knock. Then, I heard arguing. I pressed my ear against the door to hear them better.

"Who do you think you talking to?"

"I'm talking to you!"

It was the twins—Reta and Mona.

"You ain't my mama. I can do whatever I want to with my body. It's mine. You don't see me trying to tell you what to do. I don't ask you for shit so I don't expect you to volunteer it," Reta said.

"What you do don't just affect you, Reta. It affects all of us," Mona pleaded.

"Well how about I just leave then? Is that what you want?"

"I didn't say that. If you would just listen, then…"

Heavy footsteps trailed further away from the door and their voices got smaller and smaller until I couldn't hear them anymore. That also meant that I would have had to knock harder in order to be heard. Suddenly, the whole idea seemed downright ridiculous. I hadn't seen those girls in four years. What would I say when they opened the door? What would my visit mean to them? Hands down, I expected to have the door slammed in my face. But what if they welcomed me? What questions would they have and how would I answer? Would I have to start making a visit more often? I took slow steps backwards off the porch, back to my car, and drove away.

That took a toll on me and I needed some fresh air. They'd recently rebuilt the French Market so I decided to check it out, grab myself a few hot calas, a cup of coffee, and listen to the open air jazz. I was doing just that right there when I heard someone calling for me. Since I was wearing my sunglasses, I didn't expect to be noticed. I turned to see who it was and dropped my cup, splashing scorching hot coffee on my own feet and a few others. I didn't even apologize. I just took off. Since I was wearing a long skirt that day, I had to pinch the sides so I wouldn't trip.

My car was parked about two blocks away and I wasn't even halfway there before it started raining. Not sprinkling, but thundering, lightening, and pouring. The sky just opened up and let loose. I knew that it was my fault. God was punishing me for seeing my own child—Annette, my fourth and favorite—and running away. It was my second time that day and I reckon God had had enough. I turned my heater on and pulled away, apologizing to my baby girl all the way back to the house.

As if the bad weather and my mood to match wasn't enough, when I got home, the last son of a bitch that I ever wanted to see was there. Earl. He had the nerve to be sitting on my sofa with his arms stretched out across the back like he owned the place. He had a drink in his right hand and the twins sitting on each side of him. I walked over, took my glass from him, and told him to leave. I actually said a few more words than that, but to make a long story short and keep it sweet, I'll leave it at that.

He smiled, flashing those raggedy ass teeth. What he should've been trying to spend his money on is getting them teeth fixed. He stood up and spread his arms for a hug. I dodged it.

"Don't act like that, pretty baby," he cooed.

"I'ma act worse than that if you don't get up out of my house," I warned.

He smiled again, looking me over. "Money sho'll look good on you."

That was the first compliment of many to come. That one was, by far, his favorite. He would also tell me that he wasn't surprised that I'd reached the status that I had. He could always see the ambition in me. Another one was that I should be glad that we parted ways. Otherwise, I would've never tapped into the power that I possessed.

His words were saviors. I'd been locked inside of my own head, waking up and going to sleep with money on my mind. Whenever another thought or feeling arose then I was forced to kill it. I had no time or chance to take the risk. He provided a safe space for me to talk, laugh, reminisce, vent, and plan. I could be me.

"How's my baby girl?" he'd asked one day.

"She alright. They're all down there with my mama," I lied. That was the only lie that I ever had to tell. He never asked again.

He touched me like he'd lost a good woman once before. The way he kissed me gave voice to the nights that he'd said what he would do if he ever got another chance with her. His eyes said that he'd found her—again.

It all felt so good, but I still couldn't help but wiggle beneath his grasp. I was like a terrible two that just learned how to walk. I needed him to respect that I neither wanted nor needed to be carried. Ever again. I just wanted my hand held and for him to notice the little mole between my thumb and index finger. He was supposed to see the little nub beside my pinky that was once a finger. Tease me about it until I was near tears and then kiss it until it was funny again. I just wanted somebody to walk next to on life's rocky roads.

But that's not what I got. Instead, I got a man who was too used to power and control. Used to money and all that comes with it. Used to getting his way. I got a married man who refused to leave his wife, but insisted that I see no one else. A man that could throw the words man, woman, responsibilities, God, the Bible, and destiny together in such a way that had me second guessing if my proper place was indeed to stand behind him.

I never entertained that thought for too long though because it would never work. I had too much mouth to sit back and shut up. Hell, that's why I couldn't stand being a child and living up under my mama. And that's exactly why I made myself a woman at sixteen. On top of that, Earl cooked better than me, cleaned better, and just kept a better home.

I was better at the other stuff—like taking care of business. Yeah, he owned a shrimping business that made plenty of money, but that was due to an ash of luck. His uncle left him a boat when he died. Earl liked to fish so that's what he did. Somebody offered to buy his catchings one day and that's how he got started. He got the basics down—fish, catch, and sell. What he didn't get was that when you have more than one boat and when you have folk working for you, then it got a little tricky. You couldn't treat everybody the same 'cause everybody wasn't the same. And you damn sure couldn't treat everybody like you didn't need them 'cause you did. You didn't take no bullshit, no, but it was a fine line to walk, to balance it all. A good boss made for good workers.

I had to go down to that dock on more than one occasion to save his ass, whether it was from a group of pissed off workers or some pissed off customers. He recognized my strengths, even if they weren't dressed in steel toe boots, dirty denims, and calloused hands. He had to. But how was it that he could have me thinking otherwise? Had me wondering if my place was at home. He had me upset with the one person whose opinions mattered most— mine. But I couldn't stay away. Where and when would I ever find better? Earl might not have been the perfect man for me, but he was comfortable. What I came to realize though is that sometimes you had to get a little uncomfortable to learn just how big of a fool you are. It showed you that you really didn't have shit figured out like you thought you did.

A letter from my sister Etta was just the thing to snatch me out of my comfort zone. She said that our mama had suffered a stroke and was only getting worse. She didn't have much longer to live— a few days at the most. It would help if I could come down and help get things in order, make arrangements, and make sure that Mama would leave this world with her daughters at her side.

It wasn't an easy decision to make, but I decided to go ahead and go. Earl was actually the main one pushing me to go, reminding me that I only got one mama. He also told me how his daddy had lived two blocks over and only came by twice. So, he held a grudge for a long time. When it came time for his daddy to die, he refused any part of it. In the end, he only hurt himself; he could've used that time to make amends.

I heard him, but I wasn't hearing him. See, I heard that he only hurt himself and that he could've used that time to do something else. My mind filled in its own blanks. I wasn't about to hurt myself. Maureen Williams was not about to leave this earth without hearing about all the fucked up shit she ever said or did to me. If she only had a few days to live, then I was reserving a few hours of those days in advance.

I just had to figure out how I wanted to get there. Two planes had just crashed into each other in Tenerife, wherever the hell that was. Almost six hundred people died and the news people were calling it The Worst Air Disaster Ever. Needless to say, my ass wasn't getting on no airplane. Earl said that I was talking crazy, claiming that there were more car accidents than plane accidents. That didn't change my mind in the least bit. You had a chance of surviving a car accident, but a plane accident…

Riding the bus was out of the question and the train wasn't much better. Just when I was about to say forget it, Earl hired a driver for me. The car was just my kind of size and style so I had no complaints. I put Freckles in charge and gave her a month's worth of payments for my kids. Whenever I left, I sent them a little extra or as New Orleans folk would call it, a little lagniappe.

After a heated argument with Earl, because I wouldn't let him stay in the house without me being there, I was on my way.

I tried to read during the trip, but my mind was too busy to focus. I tried to sleep, but my daydreams didn't leave enough room for the real ones. I counted the trees, but somehow they reminded me of Walter and our bus ride from Coushatta to New Orleans. I struck up conversation with the driver, but he acted like he didn't get paid enough to say anything except for yes ma'am and no ma'am and to nod his peanut head every now and then. I settled on writing a list of things that I needed to say and do while I was down there.

Chapter 13

I wrote word for word what I was going to tell my mama, my sister, Girly, and Eugene. The last thing to do was to burn that damn barn to ashes. My timing could not have been any more perfect. We had made it. I didn't need an announcement to know that we had arrived. I could smell the river. I could hear the racism snickering. I could taste the grains of red clay dirt in my teeth, which was a delicacy growing up. I was back at "home" and was feeling all but that warm feeling that "home" is supposed to give you.

My nerves rattled so bad that my teeth chattered. It's not too late to turn around. No, I can't turn around. That's a coward move and I'm anything, but a coward. I took a deep breath to relax, or at least try to.

"Josephine, get yo'self together," I reasoned with myself.

Without warning, my rooted dialect had returned. Even the driver had noticed, turning around to give me an are-you-okay look. I nodded my head, assuring him that I was when I really wanted to tell him to high tail my ass back to New Orleans.

My sister pulled up in the nick of time. She was driving a white Pontiac that could have used a good sponging.

"Well, Ms. Du Bois..." said the driver.

"I know. I know. I'm going. Give me a few seconds to get my shit together, will you?"

Never let 'em see you sweat, I reminded myself. I'm Josephine Du Bois. Ms. Josephine Du Bois. I stood up and my legs felt like rubber. I grabbed the seat to level myself. With carefully measured steps and calculated breathing, I made my way to the Pontiac.

The driver loaded my Italian leather fashioned luggage into the backseat and opened the front passenger door for me. I got in and the tension stiffened times ten. She didn't even look at me, just shifted gears and pulled out the station. I began scratching my palms which was something I hadn't done in over fifteen years. She looked down at my hands and I stopped.

The car's burgundy liner was thumb tacked to the ceiling, half hanging. The seat was peeling and stabbing at my thigh like a plastic knife. I crossed my leg over the tear. Etta's glow was gone, I noticed. She looked beat, aged and tired. Puffed bags dressed her weary eyes. Strands of wired grays pouted from her hairline. Chipped polish on her nails. Nonetheless, her head was held ridiculously high with lips pursed tight—a habit she inherited from Mama.

"I see ain't nothing change round here," I said, cutting through the thick silence.

She exhaled through her nose and shook her head. Well, it was true; nothing had changed. Since I'd been born, only a city hall had managed to emerge. The sheriff and mayor stood in front of it, intently watching as we passed. The same serving sheriff and mayor since I was lil'. Coushatta only had one sheriff and only needed one. The population couldn't be no more than five hundred and that was counting the dogs.

They couldn't stand the niggas already living there, let alone any new ones. The sheriff was clearly disgusted. Evident in the way he spat on the sidewalk and twisted his face. The mayor on the other hand seemed a bit interested, curious if you will. I smiled.

We crossed the railroad tracks, the Jim Crow line, and my blood simmered a slow boil. The same reaction I'd been getting since I was the girl who'd just learned that I was to always live inferior to those on the other side because of the color of my skin, which ain't that far off from theirs. The big ole' houses, lush lawns, and paved streets faded into raggedy, shotgun houses with dirt roads and balding lawns.

We had our own riddle for this side of the tracks: The first little pig built his house out of straw. The second little pig built his house out of sticks. The third little pig built his house across the tracks, 'cause these houses over here ain't shit.

"How yo' girls?" she asked.

"Couldn't be better," I answered, knowing that I hadn't seen them in over four years. I still provided for them though, which was more than most parents could say.

We pulled up to the house and into the front yard. Houses on this side didn't have driveways. I stared at the house for a couple unmoved seconds. A tiny, blue wooden square with a triangle on top. The paint was eaten away like the paint on Etta's nails. Our house used to stand out from all others on the street that were either painted white or not painted at all. Weeds protruded from what used to be the garden out back. I reached out to open the front door and Etta grabbed my hand.

"You ain't been here to know nothing 'bout nothing. So don't go judging what you don't know. These yo roots too case you don' forgot." She clenched her jaw attempting to cease the quiver in her pursed lips. Her eyes watered and before I could respond, she went in the house leaving me and her threat staring each other down on the porch.

I looked around and sure enough the nosey assed, nothing-better-to-do neighbors were looking. Only Ms. Jessie Lee, who had come outside pretending to sweep her porch, spoke. She seemed smaller and still had the same red bandana tied around her head, house shoes on, and a smile on her face. I waved back.

147

"Whatchu got on, gal?" she yelled. I looked down at my five thousand dollar sheared chinchilla coat and felt like a clown. I smiled bashfully and went on in the house before she fired up a porch-to-porch conversation.

I walked in the house and just like that, Josephine abandoned me. Louisa had resurrected and started scratching the hell outta my palms. The house was the same as I had left it, but no longer smelled like good graciousness: savory ox tails and collards or smothered chops and grits to name a few. Instead, it smelled like sick flesh, urine, and rubbing alcohol. My stomach churned and I had to suppress the vomit riding up my throat.

Etta stomped back up front. "Can you muster up the decency to see bout yo sick mama or you too good?" she asked, looking me up and down.

"Lemme grab my bags first," I said.

The fresh air was relieving of the smell of sickness, thick tension, and painful memories. As slow as I could, I unloaded the bags from the trunk. One by one, I hauled them up the porch. They were probably inside talking about me. Didn't matter much to me though. Hell, they needed me. They called me down for help. I rehearsed my lines, my questions, and everything else I felt that my mama needed to know. All the pain she caused me, neglect as a child, favoritism she showed, and how she made me feel like the shit on the bottom of someone's shoe. I took a deep breath and walked back in.

The living room was just as I'd last seen it, only dusty. The plastic-wrapped burgundy floral sofas were still there along with the large, gold framed mirror, walled behind the big sofa. There were still the matching rugs, faux burgundy and gold plants, antique figurines atop the corner shelf, and the family bible rested on the coffee table. It was a big, white, worn bible with gold trim that held all of our names, parents, and birthdates.

I could hear Etta's voice as I neared the back of the tiny house. I tried to walk lightly, to ease the creaking of the floor, but my feet betrayed me. I was a nervous mess. With each step, I shrunk. They were in Mama's room, adjacent to the one that Etta and I shared. I went over my lines once again in my head. Mama's door was open. Etta was tending to her. I took one step in the room, not wanting to come in any further, getting in the way. Mama's king sized mahogany wood bed had been replaced with a thin, railed hospital bed. Stacks of folded cloths sat atop the dresser. The silver pans sitting next to them told me that they were diapers.

Etta discovered my presence as she walked over to the other side of the bed. Mama's back faced me, building a small wall between she and I. I felt sixteen-years-old again. I felt like running, but my feet didn't move. Only my heart started running as if it would beat its way out of my chest. *I'm 34, almost 35 years old*, I reminded myself. *And regardless of what this woman put me through, I made it. She couldn't stop me. What do I have to be afraid of?*

Etta clutched the bed sheet and prepped Mama to flip her over. To face me. Mama caught my eye the same time I caught hers and my list of things to say evaporated. I swallowed the lump in my throat and smiled shyly. The stone faced woman that I was accustomed to wasn't there. Half of her face sagged, meeting the left side of her body which sagged as well. She was nothing more than unhappy to see me. Although her face was distorted, I could still make out that she was trying to turn up her lip. Her eyes travelled down to my shoes and back up. I did the same as if I hadn't dressed myself.

I turned my attention back to Mama. She looked terrible. Her hair was all over head her head. I felt bad for her. I clenched my jaw and inhaled some courage. After all, she deserved everything that happened to her. She let out a long moan, intended to be words, but I guess the stroke distorted her speech too.

"She here to help us. I can't keep doing this by myself no mo'. You killing my back." Ella grouched. "…and my marriage," she added under her breath.

So, not only did she ask for me to come back to help with a mother who could give two shits about me growing up, but she asked for me to come back behind Mama's back. She didn't even know that I was coming. I should've put that shady shit in the spotlight. The last thing I needed was for Mama to think that I had some weak ass change of heart. No, I was asked to come.

Etta shifted all of her weight to one foot and placed her hand on her hip. "Standing there gawking ain't helping."

I cleared my throat, dismissing all the remarks that I wanted to say, and walked closer to the bed. I looked down at Mama for permission to help. She stared at the ceiling as if she didn't even know that I was standing there. Etta tossed me a soaking wet towel. Instinctively, I caught it, and then dropped it. It was probably all kinds of filth on that rag.

"Don't worry. It ain't dirty," said Etta with a smirk. "Yet."

I didn't find her little joke funny so I pretended not to hear it. I was there so I may as well helped. I was doing this for my own sake. As soon as the time was right, I was shooting off all of my questions. Even if her ass couldn't answer them, she'd get a piece of my mind. I shook off my chinchilla and draped it across the television. I went back over to the bed and dipped the rag in the pail and rung it tight. That grabbed mama's attention. She looked at what I was doing, and then up at Etta with her eyebrows scrunched together. Etta patted her shoulder. I stopped to check my freshly painted fingernails, making sure the fresh coat wasn't ruined.

"Ain't no room for all that uppity mess," Etta spat at me.

"If I'm not mistaken, you asked me to come down here," I said, rolling my neck and pointing at my chest for emphasis.

"Well if you came here to show yo ass, then just leave," Etta said with arms folded across her chest, nostrils flaring.

I held up my palms, stopping her. "You ain't said but a word." I walked over to the television, grabbed my coat, and left.

"I hope you got some walking shoes with that big ass bear coat!" she screamed.

I stormed out of the house, rattling every figurine on the shelf and every dish in the china cabinet. I slammed the door behind me. I didn't know why I any damn way. *Wasted my damn time. I could've been making money for all this shit.* I walked to the only motel in town with plans of one-waying my ass back to New Orleans first thing in the morning.

Then morning rolled around and I was still there. I was tired as all get out because I hadn't slept a lick. I didn't ride for five hours for nothing. I did it because I had something to say. I was tired of trying to forget everything that happened. Not that I could anyway. It was time for me to gone on and bring everything out of the closet so that it could be put in its proper place.

I waited until it was time to check-out before I left. I stopped for coffee at a diner around the corner. I did a lot of thinking there. I was on my third cup of coffee and had finished half of a cigar when I decided that fussing and cussing wouldn't get anything solved. It would only raise hell which would end up making me leave for real.

To be honest with myself, I guess that was what I wanted. It was fear. I had to determine what it was that I was really looking to get out of this conversation. Was I expecting an apology and if so, what would happen afterwards? Was I expecting her to act out? I had no idea. Was my expectation even important? Again, I had no clue.

What I did know was that I had a dying mother on the other side of town. I had already wasted almost 24 hours and it was no telling how much longer she had to go. It was time for me to be the woman that I was claiming to be, climb out of hiding, and gone handle business. It amazed me how the world could picture me as some big, bad wolf because I owned a gun, shot it once or twice, managed women, and dodged the law. Then, I come back to a crumb-sized town and couldn't muster the courage to face a crippled, old woman on her death bed.

I drank the last cold swallow, placed a twenty dollar bill on the table, and left. It was a misty rain outside. Not hard enough to drench me, but just enough to ruin my makeup and frizz my curls. For the month of May it was still rather nippy too. I could've easily walked back to the hotel and checked back in. It would've taken me less than five minutes to do so. Instead, I prepared myself for the twenty minute walk across the tracks, past the convenient store, three streets down, and four houses over on the left-hand side.

I marched up to the door and hesitated. Do I knock or just walk in? I decided the latter. The heat in the house hugged me like a second coat. I dropped mine on the coach in the living room and took a look at myself in the mirror that hung above the couch. My face was oily and my curls were through. I twisted my hair into a makeshift bun and pinned it in place. It would have to do.

With delicate steps, I made my way to my mother's room. It still held the same air that it did when I was child. You knocked and waited to be invited in before entering. You had better not go in there unless she specifically told you so. Even then, you only touched what she told you to get. A threatened consequence wasn't necessary. We just knew better.

I rapped the door three times lightly with my knuckles. "It's me," I called out.

"Come on in," Etta answered.

I creaked the door open, just wide enough for me to slip through and closed it behind me. The floor heater next to the dresser glowered with orange wires. I could've sworn that I could see the heat radiating from it. I loosened my top two buttons. Etta was removing Mama's nightgown so I offered to help.

"Hold her up for me."

I stood on the opposite side of the bed and pressed my palm into her cold, bony back. It knocked my breathing out of rhythm. I had to catch myself. Her hair was greyed and matted like a bird's nest that had been stomped on. Her head leaned forward as if it were trying to meet her lap. I held it back as best as I could.

"Is she sleep?" I asked.

"Something like that. It's normal for her."

Then Mama took one long inhale and I assumed that she was about to wake up. She tried to release the breath, but it sounded strained so I lifted her chin to give her room to breathe. It was no longer frightening at all. It was like caring for a baby. If I let her go, she would drop. If I shook her, she would shake.

The strained breathing turned into gurgling. I looked at Etta, not knowing what to do. She moved as if nothing had happened, pulling the flowered shirt down over Mama's head and pulling her right arm through the sleeve. She nodded her head for me to do the same with the side closest to me. I did.

"Why is she breathing like that?"

"That's called the death rattle. Just means that she ain't got much longer is all."

She spoke as if we were discussing what time she would be getting off work instead of her dying. Her bluntness was pissing me off, but I couldn't comprehend why. I just knew that I wanted her to be less harsh with her words. More kind and more hopeful. And...tears fell from both eyes, completely missing my cheeks and splashing against Mama's thighs instead. I tried to blink them away, but it only blurred my vision.

"Cheap ass mascara," I said. "Here." I laid mama down carefully and excused myself from the room.

The one bathroom in the house seemed smaller than it did when I was growing up. It still smelled faintly of ammonia, but more pissy than sterile. There were neatly folded white cloths stacked on the floor in between the toilet and the sink. The cap on the toothpaste was missing and the mirror was speckled with spit.

I felt sick and the heat was making it no better. I splashed my face with cold water and when I looked up, I saw my mother's reflection—her younger self. I jumped. My heart pounded and suddenly the room felt too small. I opened the door, but it didn't help. I splashed my face again and that helped, but only a little. I grabbed one of the cloths, wet it, and pressed it against my neck to cool me down while taking long, deep breaths. It helped.

I walked back into Mama's room with the cloth resting on the back of my neck. Etta looked up briefly, back to her book, and then right back up at me. She shook her head and laughed.

"What's so funny?"

"You. What's that on yo' neck back there?" she asked.

I shrugged. "One of those towels sitting next to the sink."

"More like one of those diapers, you mean?"

I snatched it off of my neck and jumped back from it. You would've thought that it was a cockroach. I cussed under my breath, picked the damn thing up, and tossed in the bin on the other side of the room. One chair sat next to the bin.

Etta was still reading and I didn't have anything to give my attention to. I couldn't talk to Mama, because she wasn't in the position to do no kind of talking or listening. The TV was dusted over and it wasn't no sense in turning it on since it really wasn't nothing I cared to watch anyway. I wondered if Etta was really reading. I mean, can you actually get into a story when your twin sister, who you ain't seen in damn near 20 years, was sitting right next to you? And, when your dying mother was right next to her?

"Happy birthday," she said.

"Happy birthday? It ain't today is it? Please don't tell me it's today."

"Unless we can move time backward or foreword, then it's today alright. May 17th."

"Shit," I muttered. "Well, happy birthday to you too. What you got planned?"

She took a deep breath. "I ain't celebrated a birthday in God knows how long. Just another day around here."

"Well ain't your husband taking you out or something?" I asked innocently then realized soon after how nosey it sounded.

"Nah, not this time."

We just sat there after that. No one said anything. I was sure that hours were passing by, but there was no clock. It was as if I'd sacrificed the one thing that I knew best: numbers—time and money. At that moment, it felt like neither one mattered. It got me nervous a little bit. My hands and my feet got restless. My scalp itched; my bra felt too tight; and the cocoa butter on my legs was melting or something. On top of feeling sweaty, I was feeling greasy.

I stood up and stretched. I opened my mouth to ask if Etta wanted me to bring something to eat back or something. I had to get out of there. Then, Mama's breathing quieted. I'd become immune to how loud and ragged it had been. She made several weak attempts to cough and opened her eyes. Her left eye sagged along with her jaw and the left side of her mouth. Drool seeped from the corner.

Seeing me, her right eye lowered, almost matching the left. She stared at me. Just stared at me. She didn't look me up and down or roll her eyes. She just stared at me. The only thing that moved was her chest, rising and falling. I kept my eyes on her as well. I wanted to explain to her that I was no longer a child. She needed me now and I would not tolerate the disrespect. I had some talking to do and in her position, she had no choice but to hear me out. I explained this without opening my mouth. I said it all with the blackest part of my eye and not once did I blink.

Etta granted me the very moment that I was waiting for when she too stood up. "Well, good morning," she said to Mama.

Mama grunted in response.

"You want some oatmeal or some grits?" Etta asked.

Again, Mama grunted.

"You gotta eat, Mama. Now either you pick or I'ma pick."

She grunted again, louder.

"Grits it is. I ain't about to be going back and forth with you today. While Louisa heat 'em up, I'ma gone change you."

I wasn't used to taking directions. I was usually the one giving them so it took me a few seconds to realize that I was supposed to be halfway to the kitchen instead of standing there like a fool. I put on a pot of water and waited for it to begin to boil. It would take a while to cook since, unlike the rest of the world, Mama didn't believe in instant grits; she wanted stoneground grits mixed with salt, pepper, butter, cheese, and a little milk so they'd be creamy.

I toyed with the magnets on the refrigerator while I waited. There was one of the New Orleans Crescent City Bridge. She'd had it since forever. There was a short list of phone numbers stuck to the fridge with a magnetic bottle of Tabasco. Then there was the cross, a white Jesus, a red letter K, a pig ready to eat barbecue, a calendar dated for seven years ago, and a stick person that Etta had made as a child.

The drawer right next to the refrigerator was filled with cookbooks: country cookbooks, gourmet cookbooks, Sunday morning cookbooks, pies and cakes, and one that Etta had made in the third grade. I looked for mine, but it wasn't there. I took everything out of the drawer, put it back, gone through the rest of the drawers, but it wasn't there.

I went to the living room and pulled out three big, heavy brown books full of photos. I flipped through every single one. There was only one of Mama as a child. She had three ponytails, was holding a doll, and looked like you couldn't have paid her to smile. There were a few others of her as an adult; they were mainly church pictures. Some of random people that I couldn't call out.One of Maman in her coffin. I was surprised that it had been taken. Maman didn't believe in having her picture taken. She claimed that it stole your soul.

Etta was on damn near every other shot and then I finally found one of myself—in the corner of a picture focused on Etta. Half of my body was cut out of the picture and, in the back, on a tacky orange sofa sat a man holding a beer. He was as yellow as Etta, had curly hair, slender limbs, and the flash made his eyes red. Just like Etta's. In fact, they looked a lot alike. Just alike. I pulled the picture out, folded it, and stuffed it in my bra.

That was just the fire that I needed. I stormed back into the room to find Etta leaned over Mama. Her mouth was pressed against Mama's. Her left hand sat on top of her right hand and she was thrusting at the center of Mama's chest. She yelled for me to call someone, but my hearing faded. My sense of feeling went next and then my sight and then my ability to stand.

Chapter 14

My mama was dead. Dead as in unable to respond and never coming back. The house and yard had filled with a good third of Coushatta's entire population. Every single black person that had good enough health to stand was there. It wasn't your typical death gathering though. Nobody needed their back rubbed or their tears wiped away or to hear that she didn't have to suffer anymore because she was in a much better place. We were fine.

Etta had shed a few tears, but she wasn't nearly as hysterical as I would have imagined her to be. Her reasoning was that she knew the day was coming and had had plenty of time to prepare herself for it. Me? I just felt stuck. I didn't get the chance to speak a word on what I needed to say. The main person that needed to hear it was no longer available.

As silly as it sounded, I couldn't help but think that Mama had did that shit on purpose. She felt it coming and went ahead and rolled out. Freckles often played the mediator in the house. Whenever someone was acting pissy, she would ask them: "What do you really want right now?" At that very second, I wanted to wake my mama up and tell her what I had to say. But I couldn't. As much money that I had and the power that the money brought with it, there wasn't a damn thing that I could buy or one person that I could call to bring her back. Therefore, I felt stuck.

I wasn't on the verge of cussing nobody out or nothing like it. My blood wasn't boiling. It was more of a slow simmer. My heat had been turned down from high to low, but that didn't mean that it wasn't worth paying attention to. Low ain't the same thing as off. It was still heat and could still burn. I didn't want to get to that point though. I'd been there and knew that nothing good came from it. I also knew that if I didn't do something with it right there on that porch, then I was going to be stuck with it and would end up burning someone that had nothing to do with it.

The bushes next to the house shook and then stopped. I looked over at Etta, but her gaze was fixed on the street up ahead. I cocked my head to the side and looked back over at the bush to determine whether I'd heard right or if the white lightening had snuck up on me. I grabbed an ice cube out of my glass and threw it at the bush. A black cat jetted across the yard.

"Gone on now. Ain't no more room for bad luck round here," I said.

"You sound just like Mama," said Etta.

"Don't compare me to her," I said, feeling my nostrils flare. "Do not compare me to that woman."

"That sound like something she would've said too," Etta added.

"Well she didn't. I did and let that be the last of it."

She chuckled and I realized that I was sounding more and more like her with every word that tumbled from my lips. Far more than my mother's superstitions had rubbed off on me. I'd tried my damnedest not to be anything like her—so much that I spun completely around. Now, looking in the mirror, I saw her— only she wore my nose, eyes, and mouth. I was the exact opposite of her: fearless, loud, black and proud, having a mind of my own, well-traveled, and filthy fucking rich. I refused to just sit back and accept that I was doomed to any way of life. You always had a choice.

"Just because she chose to live her life by default, it wasn't nobody's fault but her own. The real reason she didn't like me was because I wasn't like you, Etta. I could see through her bullshit. She couldn't shape my mind like it was raw dough waiting to be baked. I've always had a mind of my own. Always."

Etta didn't respond and I was grateful for it. I really hadn't meant for those words to be spoken. They were nothing more than unruly thoughts. That didn't mean that they weren't true though because they were. We did have a choice and my choice was to have a say so in how I lived. I was not about to sit back, suffer, and point blame. I wanted out of Coushatta, so I got out. I wanted money, so I did what I had to do to get it.

It sounded good and not long ago, I would've pointed at the me today and said, "that's exactly who I want to be." But knowing what I know now, I'd have to say not so much. Having a whole lot doesn't mean a whole lot and that's the truth so help me God. While my mama sat on one end of the pole, I sat at the other. But the end ain't where you want to be. It's the middle. The ends were too worrisome a place. You have and then you have not. Your downs outweigh your ups and then your downs ain't never just regular downs; they're the scraping, scratching, and crawling kind of down—the kind that's bad enough to stop your heart.

The middle is where you find the happy that lasts. Don't get me wrong, there are rich people in the middle. I'm just not one of them. My goal was to be there one day. The conversation with my mama was supposed to push me five steps closer to being there, but hey, I guess we couldn't always get what we wanted. Since talking to Mama was no longer an option, I was gonna have to find another way to deal with it. Otherwise, I would die just like her— spoiled. Not the bratty kind of spoiled. I'm talking about sweetness turned sour, blackened, and rotted from the inside out.

"What you over there thinking about?" Etta asked.

"You wouldn't understand."

"We came from the same womb, damn near at the same time. If anybody will understand, it's me."

"We might've been born side by side, but we weren't raised like that. So like I said, you wouldn't understand. Mama had my mind so messed up, it ain't even funny."

"Now, hold on. Mama did the best she could with what she had."

"Ain't that just like you to say? But I ain't surprised. Not in the least."

"Louisa, lemme tell you something."

"I don't need you to tell me a damn thing. I'm a grown woman and through all the bullshit, I've done pretty damn good for myself. Better than anyone else around here."

"I'm glad you mentioned it. Now with that being said, don't you think that you've been playing this victim role a little too long?"

"The victim?"

"Yes, *the victim*. Pointing the finger, pushing the blame, and putting women into the same box of hurt that you yourself was forced into. For the life of me, I don't get that."

"And you wouldn't understand, Etta. You were Mama's favorite. You could do no wrong. You didn't have to hear how fucked up you were, how you were a mistake, and how you would never be nothing."

"Exactly. I got the opposite. I dived headfirst into this world right here thinking I could do no wrong. You don't think that had its downfall? You think I just moseyed my way through life with not a bump or a bruise?"

"Not like I did and that's for damn sure."

"Now what I ain't about to do is sit up on this porch with you and compare whose hurt was the worst. We all hurt. I don't care what color you is, if you a man or a woman, rich or poor. What matters is how you deal with it."

I rolled my eyes. "Well since you got it all figured out, tell me all about it. I ain't got shit else to do."

"You want to know what I figured out? Huh? I learned that we'll never have it all figured out because we ain't meant to. All we meant to do is live, learn, and pass it down to make life easier for the next ones. That's it."

I leaned back for show. "You figured all that out? Girl, you should write a book."

"Louisa, you'll make somebody slap the plum shit outta you."

"I guess that's the one thing we got in common then."

"Must be and ain't that something? Came from the same womb, minutes apart, and ain't nothing alike."

"Not a lick."

Neither of us spoke for a while after that. We sat there holding our jars of white lightening, listening to the crickets chirp. I forgot how still the night life could be. There weren't any cars passing, no music blaring, no French Quarter or bordellos. The one nightclub that Coushatta did have died down right around the time that Bourbon Street comes alive.

"I'd be lying though, if I didn't say that I was a little curious of what happened in them kinds of places."

"What places you talking about?" I asked, knowing full well what she was talking about. I just wanted to hear her say it.

She leaned over and whispered, "Whorehouses. You don't think I watch the news?"

I threw my head back and laughed. "You wouldn't believe me if I told you."

Her eyes got big. "Try me."

"What you wanna know?"

She shrugged. "What's the craziest thing ever happen?"

"Honey, my world revolves around crazy."

"Well tell me something. Anything."

"Let's see," I said, really thinking. "Not too long ago, I had to chase a woman off of my porch with a baseball bat. She thought her husband was there."

"Was he?" she asked.

"No, he wasn't," I answered, telling half of the story. She didn't need to know that it was Earl's wife.

"Tell me something else. I know you got something juicier than that."

"You know Charlie Rogers?"

"The white man that played in the westerns?"

I nodded my head. "He called himself wanting two of my girls at the same time. Usually that ain't no problem, but the two he wanted were sisters. Twins, as a matter of fact. We told him no and he cut up. I ain't talking about cussing and fussing either. He ran in the bathroom, locked the door, and said he was never coming out. Got to crying and carrying on, the whole nine. I had to threaten to call the police on him."

"You weren't really gonna do it though was you?"

"Like hell I wasn't. I'ma citizen and pay taxes just like everybody else."

"I thought it was illegal."

"Well it is." I didn't want to tell her that I went ahead and put a few officers on my payroll to keep their damn mouths shut. "It's too much to explain, but yeah, I can call, too."

"Wow," she said. "So whatever happened to Charlie? How did y'all get him out the house?"

"Luckily, we had a head doctor in the house at the time."

The face she made asked the question that her mouth didn't have to. I went ahead and answered it. "He was there as a customer."

"Oh okay. Now go ahead…"

"Anyways, he asked a few questions and learned that he was a mama's boy. So, he basically used that against him, reminding him that his mama wouldn't be too proud of him when she found out that her son had lost his career because he'd been arrested after being caught in a whorehouse."

"And that worked?"

I nodded. I ran through a couple of more stories until I was more than sure that midnight had passed, our birthdays were over, and the next day had come. We'd grown as quiet as the town and a few times there, I had dozed off.

"I love you, Louisa. You might go by Josephine now, but to me, you still Louisa," she said, breaking the silence. "And Mama might not have said it, but she did too."

I nodded my head and began to rock. I loved my sister too. My mouth just couldn't say it. And Lord knows that I missed her. It was so many days and nights that I would wonder what she was doing, who she was with, what she was wearing, where she was living, and if she was thinking of me too. I wanted to invite her down to New Orleans to visit, take her shopping, and treat her to some of the finest dining. But I knew she wouldn't come because Mama would never approve. So, I didn't even bother wasting my time calling.

"Even though I never met them, I love my nieces too. I don't know what kind of relationship you have with 'em, but God just placed it on my heart to tell you not to let pride or fear ruin a good thing. One day your girls will go on and have kids of they own and whether you believe it or not, your story will make a difference in that line of baby making."

She'd gone too far. She'd crossed over into territory that she hadn't been invited into and it wasn't sitting right with me. I shifted my weight over to the right and then over to the left again, but that wasn't enough. It was time for her to go. I finished my drink and set it down beside my chair.

She did the same and then stood up and stretched, yawning. "Well, I reckon I better get on cross these tracks 'fore the sun come up. You know menfolk. I do it once and he'll think he can do it twice." She chuckled to herself. She stood up and leaned back with her hands on her hips. Her back cracked in at least three places.

She said that she would be back before supper the next day and then pulled off, leaving a trail of red clay dust behind her. I watched her bright red taillights until they disappeared. She was going home, across the train tracks, to what used to be the white side of town. She'd always said that she would live over there one day and she did it. She also said that she would marry a doctor and did that too. Her journey to get there and the everyday living of it was another story. Even though she hadn't told me the story, I knew that it hadn't exactly lived up to her expectations. It wasn't all that it was hyped up to be. I didn't know if I knew that simply because I was a woman and could feel them kinds of things or if it was because we shared the same womb at the same time.

I sat out for another half hour or so remembering everything that I'd either forgotten or tried to forget. There were some things that I didn't want to remember, like how Deacon Russell would make his rounds to the sick and shut-in. I swear that our street had more sick than I could stand. He was always either at the house on the left, the one on the right, the one across the street, or down the street. Somehow we always made eye contact, even if I was just peeking out of my blinds, and he would grin in that nasty way that only a low-down, dirty bastard could. If I could trade every dollar that I had to my name in exchange for my innocence back, I would. The money, I could make back in no time. Those memories, on the other hand, would never die. I could still feel his hot breath on my face, his heavy hands rummaging inside of my shirt, and his *thing* poking around my thighs trying to find its way inside.

I remember my mama's old boss lady—I couldn't recall her name for the life of me—and how she would drop Mama off sometimes. Even as a child, I hated how proper Mama would try to talk around her and how big of a smile Mama would paint on her face. I hated how Mama begged to keep her job when she got fired. I hated how she blamed me for it, saying that I should've never come up there. I only went up there because I was sick and needed my mother. She didn't complain when Etta went up there. In fact, she blessed her, claiming that God had answered her prayers by letting her off early since her back was hurting. And Etta was faking. I was really sick. Then too, the time between me going up to her job and her getting fired was at least two or three months a part. I hated how Mama would bring home hand-me-down clothes from the white folks and expect us to wear them. I remember feeling like someone was watching me, turning my head, and catching Mama looking at me like I was the one who'd pumped her with two kids and hauled ass.

Eugene was the only one who would listen to my whining and bickering. Thinking of him led me to remembering the time that Eugene ran in on me and Walter. I'd never forget the look on his face. To this day, it made me feel like the grime under a man's toilet seat. If I could go back in time, I would choose Eugene's simple ass over every flutter that Walter ever planted in my belly. His nickname wasn't Trouble Man for nothing and in the end, he was the one to die when it was so close to being me. I wrote his family to explain what happened and never got a response.

I'm more than sure that the only person in the house that could read was Girly and she couldn't even read all that good. So I made sure that I used easy words and kept it short and to the point. He was on drugs and died. I couldn't afford to bury him so the city was taking care of it. Still, no response. *She can't possibly hate me that much.* I couldn't understand back then, but it was as clear as a good batch of moonshine now. Girly confided in me that Walter raped her and did things that are too horrible to repeat. I didn't believe her. I accused her of being jealous. Looking back, I can't blame her for not caring if he died. Hell, she probably wished that I would've died with him.

It was still on my list to visit them both—Eugene and Girly. That is, if they were still living or still in town. Etta said that they were. Still living in the same old house. The old man that Girly lived with died and left her with a little money. She spent that plus some and loss the house to her debts. Eugene retired from the Army, but decided to move back home to take care of everybody else's lazy behind.

I went by, but didn't knock. I wouldn't have known what to say. So, I did what I knew how to do best. I left a few hundred dollars inside the screen door and walked away. I didn't go back to my mother's house. I just kept walking. I took a stroll downtown on Main Street where two new boutiques, a thrift store, and a pizza joint had opened. I passed the post office and stopped in front of the city hall where I'd spoke to Walter for the very first time. Our conversation was still fresh in my memory. The giddiness that I felt over two decades ago returned. I blushed at the thought of his smile and infinite coolness. His audacity and the larger-than-life air that he delivered into every room that he graced. Before the darker memories had time to surface and overshadow the brighter ones, I blew a kiss into the wind and continued my stroll.

My next stop was the Old Red River Bridge. I couldn't stop the darker memories there, and I didn't try. I reflected on the big, white Cadillac with its little, white woman on the inside. The look on Walter's face as he made love to her. My feelings of betrayal, shame, and anger. The tear in my heart that I *knew* could never be repaired. Bandaged, maybe, but fixed? Never. I recited the vow that I'd made that night: I would never again give another person that much power over me. I chuckled at the irony of that vow. No, I didn't give another person that power; I gave it back to Walter, the very one who'd abused it to begin with.

I passed the big, old house on the hill that my mama once cleaned from top to bottom on her hands and knees six days a week for pennies on the dollar. There was a young couple sitting on a swing on the wraparound porch. They were drinking what looked to be ice, cold sweet tea, but it really wasn't no telling. They didn't wave or speak. They just looked at me as I made my way down the street.

I stopped at a green street sign that read Godsley Road. That wasn't always the name of that street. I couldn't put my finger on the original name, but I knew that Godsley wasn't it. I stooped down to read the concrete post below the street sign. **In honor of Reverend John A. Godsley, our modern-day saint.** I laughed, out loud, at the thought that he was once my saint as well—my best paying customer.

More beautiful homes and a new country club dotted my path through the once forbidden side of town. If you weren't going to work or coming from work, then Blacks had no business on that side of the tracks. Times were changing. Slowly, but surely. Not only could a black woman take a leisure stroll through the neighborhood, but could purchase a house there as well. Etta was a prime example.

I crossed the infamous tracks and made a left instead of keeping straight. I passed the huge plot of land that was dressed in red clay instead of grass. An empty trash can, an upside down chitling bucket, and a pair of old shoes served as makeshift bases. I pictured clusters of kids meeting for matches of kickball, baseball, and whatever other game they could make a name and rules for. I passed a raggedy, abandoned shack next to that. Then, a little further down was the graveyard that now housed the late Marie Williams.

Chapter 15

I turned back around and went home. I wasn't mentally prepared to enter the gates where my mama had been buried only two days before. The way that my nerves crept into the pit of my stomach, you would've thought that she was rocking in a chair, waiting on me instead of lying in a closed casket that rested beneath six feet of dirt.

The funeral and burial was fine. There were people there. Etta had sizzled my hair bone straight, my makeup was flawless, and my style of dress would've turned First Lady Carter and Queen Elizabeth's face green. Who the Mardi Gras Indians were to New Orleans is who I was to Coushatta. It was obvious that I'd spent good money and time on my masks. I was someone to be marveled at. I made wannabes mad and onlookers stare. That's exactly the role that I'd grown accustomed to and enjoyed so much.

Being alone was a different case. Loneliness don't care that your hair is free of kinks. How heavy your perfume is. Where you bought your dress or how much money you spent on your shoes. Loneliness is the master of making all of that feel like nothing at all. It'll turn the radio and television on and busy your body in order to keep the thoughts away. When you least expect, it'll tap you on the shoulder and remind you of all the fucked up shit that you ever did. If you ain't careful, it'll have you defending yourself. Out loud.

But I couldn't let that deter me. I'd been faced with a challenge and if I didn't beat it then I'd never let myself live it down. Mama may have dodged what I had to say while she was here on this earth, but what she wasn't about to do was dodge me while she was up under it.

So, when Etta called to see if I wanted to have coffee with her, I politely declined. I told her that I was a little under the weather and planned to take it easy for the day. I did everything but. Instead, I took my time pinning my hair up into a simple bun. I went light with the makeup, choosing a little foundation, some mascara, and a swipe of my red lipstick. I dabbed my Miss Balmain's behind my ear and on my wrists. Clipped on my gold earrings and snapped a thin gold bracelet around my wrist to match my yellow dress and cream-colored sandals—I hated when people termed it "off-white." Nothing about me was off.

For breakfast, I took it back to my McPherson days and had an Irish Whiskey. The whiskey gave the coffee a nice kick and the coffee gave the whiskey a nice touch. It was the perfect marriage. It also got me ready to go and gave me the courage that I needed. Afterwards, I washed the cup, placed it back in its proper place, and prayed that the buzz would hold me over.

It didn't.

By the time that I'd made it back to the graveyard, I was sweating like it was one o'clock in the afternoon instead of nine o'clock in the morning. My fingernails were so deep into my palms that it surprised me to see no blood there. With the legs of a child that had been told to go get a switch, I made my way through the dead silent maze of tombstones and flowers.

There were graves that indicated that the person inside had lived over a hundred years and others told that it was the home of a child. I stopped at one that had no name or birthdate. An initial was marked as A.P. and the death date read 1863 which meant that A.P. had been a slave. I may not have finished school, but Sister Clare made sure that all of her students knew that slavery ended in 1865. Every year, she would remind us how many years ago 1865 was. In 1955, for example, she told us that slavery had ended 90 years ago and that Sister June was 96 years old.

It wasn't until I was standing in front of that grave marked for 1863 that all of Sister Clare's teachings and reminders hit me. Even then, in 1977, 1865 wasn't that long ago. It was only 112 years ago that blacks were property instead of people. I silently prayed to the body that was identified as A.P. I thanked him (or her) and congratulated him on finally being free.

By memory, I found my way to Maman's grave. I dusted it off and considered sitting before realizing that I had nothing to say. I really didn't know her. I knew her as a child, yes, but that was almost twenty-five years ago. I remembered that people loved her and that she loved me. I remembered her scratching and greasing my itchy scalp until I fell asleep. Her sweet potato pie was second to none and she would crack my pecans for me. She smiled at me like I was something worth smiling at and showed me off like I was something worth bragging on. I recall going to her house one day and seeing her sitting on the couch beaming.

"Guess where I been today?" she'd challenged me.

To this day, I don't know the source of my answer. "Mississippi."

She smiled real big, grabbed my cheeks, and started kissing all over my face, praising me for guessing right. She'd gone to visit family that we had there and had won a few dollars in some game. I chuckled, now realizing that the game was gambling. I tried to surface more memories, but other than her funeral, none would come. That was it. Instead of being sad about that, I accepted it for what it was, thanked her for loving me, and kept it moving.

The next stop was the final stop. It was the site of Maman's daughter and me and Etta's mother. Who her father was, I'll never know. Who me and Etta's was, I'll never know. I dismissed the questionable fathers as thoughts that didn't matter. What did matter was what happened over the next few minutes. Either I would finally find closure or I would live out the rest of my days without ever having it—whatever that meant.

The bundle of sunflowers that Etta had placed on her grave were still there, still fresh. She said that they were her favorite. The same bitter tongue that I had while growing up in Coushatta had returned after she said it. It was like a reflux of acid that spewed from my throat and rested on my tongue, burning and waiting to be spat on the next person that dared to piss me off. I had not one clue what our mama's favorite anything was and I doubted if she knew any of mine.

I took a deep breath, choosing to forget that moment and focus on the one at hand. I placed my bouquet of sunflowers next to Etta's and laid out a blanket to sit on. For a while, I said nothing. I just sat there. I watched the wind blow dirt and leaves into miniature tornados. I thought about what I was missing out on back home in New Orleans. I wondered what Etta was doing. For the weeks that I'd been back, we'd been spending nearly every woken moment together. She tried to teach me how to cook and I tried to teach her how to dress. If we weren't doing that, then we were either drinking, gossiping, catching up, or watching the stories.

I looked out over the graveyard and pictured all of the bodies that rested there. Not in their decayed form, but as they did on the day of their funerals. I imagined men and women dressed in their Sunday's best with their eyes closed and wondered if an afterlife truly did exist. Did their souls fly away to heaven or hell? Did it die along with the body? Enter the body of a newborn? Or, was it trapped inside of a useless shell? I guess the only way of knowing would be to die.

I traced my finger along the stem of one of the sunflowers and realized that I was beating around the bush. I focused my eyes on the crown of the grave and it didn't feel like there was a useless shell inside. It felt like she was looking right back at me. Her mouth was fixed in its usual stubborn way and she wanted me to get on with what I had to say so that she could get back to resting.

"Are you still in there?" I asked.

No response.

"I mean, I know your body in there, but are *you* in there?"

Still, no response.

"You some kind of fool," I muttered to myself.

I imagined her laughing. I would have never down-talked myself like that in front of her. The only reason that I could do it then was because she was dead. She was dead, meaning that all she had was a past. She had neither a present nor a future, but I did. Because I did and she didn't, I refused to allow her to keep the upper hand.

"You hear that? You dead. Not me. It's over for you. You lived a shitty fifty-five years in fear. I get it now. You were scared. Scared to leave this city, scared to want more for yourself, and you were scared of me because you knew that I wasn't scared. Ain't that right?" I asked, but I didn't wait on a response or a feeling. "That's why you treated me like shit and wanted me to feel like shit. Because I wasn't scared, but Etta was and that's why she was your crown and joy. I was a child. A child! There wasn't a damn thing that I could have possibly done to make you hate me that much. Nothing! But I get it now. You knew that I would go on to do something that you could never do which is live and dammit, I've been living like you wouldn't believe.

"I have money. Remember that white lady, whose behind you used to kiss? You know, the one whose house you used to clean? Well, I got her kind of money. The long kind. The kind that allows me to pay people to do what I don't feel like doing, shop until my feet hurt, travel all over this globe, eat whenever and wherever I want to, and still not run out.

"I could have helped you. I could have made your last few years on this Earth worth living, but you were too damn stuck on yourself. Whenever I needed you, you pushed me away. I asked you to take your own granddaughters in—your bloodline—just for a minute or two, while I regrouped. What did you do? You hung up in my face. Any possibility of us allowing bygones to be bygones was gone at that point. But who am I kidding? I'm pretty sure that you could not care less."

I definitely felt some energy at that point. Red, hot emotions flying all over the place like a million rubber bands pulled tight and let go. I'd gotten so upset that I'd wet the front of my dress with tears. I was sure that I looked a mess, having mascara running down my face and snot threatening to drip from the tip of my nose. My eyes were too blurry to see and they burned. I cleaned them as best as I could with the blanket and got up to leave.

My intentions were on going back to the house and taking a nap. Instead, I stopped at Church Street. I stood in the middle of the street for about a minute or two, contemplating whether or not I wanted to turn. A truck pulled up beside me and the driver asked if I needed a ride. I declined and decided to go ahead and make the turn before I brought anymore unnecessary attention to myself.

The walk was longer than I remembered. Every Sunday morning, the three of us would walk to church with our bibles tucked under our arms. A fellow church member would usually take us back home. I paused in front of the small, white dwelling. It was structured just as a child would draw a building, having a triangle sitting on top of a square. The only thing that had changed over the years was a sign out front that announced the topic of the following Sunday's sermon.

The grass was freshly cut and the building had not a speck of dirt on it. That church was cared for as if it were heaven itself. Some folk took more pride in the Lord's house than they did their own house. I cut across the lawn and went to the back. Further back, toward the woodline sat the barn. Grass and weeds that stood high enough around it to say that if they could afford to bulldoze the damn thing, they would, but since they couldn't, they would just let the grass hide it.

A snake could've been in that grass, but I couldn't let the mere chance of a snake being in there be   the end of my journey. I had to at least see. I picked up a rock and threw it in the weeds, but nothing moved. I put on my big girl panties and trudged through the tall, itchy blades and pulled open the door. It took some muscle, but I got it open. I half-expected to find a body there, but there was none. The barn held an old, stale smell to it and the windows were the kind of dirty that couldn't be cleaned. It also seemed much smaller than I remembered. Had I been wearing heels, my head would have touched the roof. Other than that, all else was the same. The same old splintered benches were there and it was as if nothing had changed. Like, at any moment, Deacon Russell would come crawling out of the church to get some.

I spread the blanket out onto the bench and took a seat. I opened my legs to let a breeze pass through. It was hotter than hell on fire. After that, I definitely planned on going back to the house. No stops or turns would dare tempt me. I craved a bath, a glass of ice water, and a cold pillow like I hadn't had one in years. I promised myself just that—as soon as I finished my business in the barn, that is. Deacon Russell was dead and there were too many plots and it was too damn hot to go looking for him, so the barn was going to have to do.

"I was a child," I said, breaking the silence. "I guess you could say that I knew better, but then again, I didn't. I was only going off of what I was told and Girly was the one telling me everything. This ain't to blame her though because, well, I should've had a mother to tell me right from wrong."

I took a deep breath to calm my nerves. My right leg bounced up and down as I fought, in vain, to keep the tears away. I'd handled my business with my mama back at the graveyard. The barn didn't have anything to do with her. As much as I wanted to believe that, it wasn't true. It did have something to do with her. It had everything to do with her.

What happens to your daughters has everything to do with you.

Knowing damn well that no one was in that barn with me, I looked around anyway. The voice had been clear as day. It was a woman's voice, but it wasn't mine and it wasn't anyone that I knew. The tone had been subtle but sure as if it knew everything about me, but needed the proper time and place to speak to me— when I was alone, sober, and couldn't deny or drown out what I'd heard. It was as if the words had been spoken from God. The hairs on my arms and neck stood to attention. I crossed my legs and ran my hands up and down my arms.

I felt myself opening up, readying to breakdown, but I didn't want to. I wanted to leave, but I couldn't. Technically, I didn't even try. I didn't uncross my legs in order to plant my feet on the ground so that I could stand. Something inside of that barn wouldn't allow me to. It wasn't aggressive at all though. Like a loving grandmother, it held me, rocked me, rubbed my back, and encouraged me to let it all out.

And I did. I cried until the wells behind my eyes ran dry. Until I could barely open my lids and my neck had to strain to keep my head up. Until the day had become night and the moon was my only source of light. Until I was so parched and in need of nourishment that my hands rattled and my legs fell weak. Until the barn went pitch black.

Chapter 16

The pillow that my head rested on was soft and cool. My covering was too heavy to be anything but handmade. The window unit hummed. The smell of a Sunday morning's breakfast invaded my nostrils. My stomach growled. I opened my eyes. I was lying in Etta's old bed in the same room that I'd grown up in. I was dressed in my sapphire satin pajama set.

I slid my feet into a pair of pink slippers that sat near the door. They fit perfectly. I walked into the kitchen and was greeted by Etta who was entertaining Eugene over a cup of coffee. He looked at me as if I had returned from the dead. I thought about how my hair and face must have looked. I turned around and dashed to the bathroom.

My hair was matted to my head and I had dried spittle on the side of my face. I turned on the bathtub faucets and while the water ran, I brushed my teeth and combed my hair back. Someone knocked on the door as I undressed.

"I'll be out in a minute," I called out.

"I was just making sure that you're okay," Etta responded and then opened the door and peeked her head inside. My face must have said it all. "I apologize. I just wanted to catch you before you got in the tub. You're not mad about..." She nodded her head toward the kitchen. "...being here, are you?"

"Should I be?" I asked.

"Not at all," she answered. "He was the one who found your butt in that barn. What were you doing in there anyway?" she asked.

"Long story, but for now, I just want to wash my behind."

"Alright, well breakfast is done and I just put on a fresh pot of coffee. Don't let it go cold," she warned.

After freshening up and determining that I looked at least halfway decent, I made my way back to the kitchen. Eugene was still there. Etta was at the sink washing dishes. I settled for a bowl of grits and a cup of coffee—black with just a spoon of sugar. I took a seat at the kitchen table directly across from him.

"Good morning," he said, speaking first.

"Good morning," I answered, blowing my grits.

"How you f-f-feeling?"

"I'm alright. How are you?"

"I c-c-can't complain."

"Eugene, tell her about the new business you got going on up in Shreveport," Etta said, drying her hands off on a towel.

He waved at her. "Ah, that ain't much of nothing. Plus, I don't w-w-wanna bore Louisa. She just sat down."

"I ain't doing nothing, but eating grits. Gone tell me about it," I encouraged him.

He grinned and wiped at the back of his neck with a handkerchief. "I bought a f-f-few plots of land. Not much, about four acres all together."

"Well what you plan on doing with 'em Eugene," Etta asked with her hand on her hip.

"R-r-reckon I'll turn one into a graveyard since folk ain't gon' n-n-never stop dying. Then, I'ma build a filling station at the other two."

"Sounds like a good idea to me," I said and then spooned a heap of grits into my mouth.

"I'm trying," he said.

"I need to run home for a second. I'll be back in about an hour," Etta said, grabbing her purse from the chair.

I tried giving her the eye, but she ignored me. She was gone before I could say something. That left me to entertain Eugene, who looked far too comfortable. I finished my breakfast and got up to rinse my bowl out. Steam was still rising from the coffee pot so I decided to pour myself another cup.

"Care for more coffee," I offered.

He picked his mug up and extended it towards me. Just as I was opening my mouth to ask, he told me that he preferred his black, no sugar or cream. I sat down and placed both cups back on the table. He picked his up and took a long sip. Afterwards, he looked at me and smiled.

During the silence, I wondered who had gotten to the two hundred dollars that I left in the screen door. I recalled how he used to stare at me in school. That is, until he was old enough to work and had to drop out. He was still my friend though. I didn't tease him about his stuttering problem like the other kids did and even though he smelled bad I didn't throw it in his face. I don't know what I saw in that boy. That coughed a chuckle out of me.

"What's so funny?" he asked, smiling.

"Nothing," I lied.

"Oh. You don' got m-m-married again yet?"

"Nope."

"I don't b-b-believe it. A woman as handsome as you is."

"Handsome? Men are handsome. Women are beautiful."

"A woman can be handsome too."

"Hmpf. Not this one," I said, drinking the last of my coffee.

"You always was a f-f-firecracker."

"What you mean by that?" I asked, rolling my neck.

"I-I-I didn't mean no harm by it. You just say what's on your m-m-mind. That's all."

"Well if I don't say what's on my mind, who else gon' say it?" I asked.

We both laughed. It was a good laugh. The kind that make you sigh when you're through. Either Etta had spiked my coffee or Eugene didn't look as bad when he laughed. His eyes chinked which made me notice how long and thick his eyelashes were. His skin was dark as oil and just as smooth—just like Walter's had been. His lips were full and fit his face well. A good haircut and a new outfit was really all he needed.

"I missed you, Louisa."

That caught me off guard. It made me swallow down the wrong pipe and choke. He got up to help and I held my hand up, signaling that I was fine. I cleared my throat and apologized for my minor interruption.

"So what do you do for fun around here?" I asked.

"Was Trouble Man a b-b-better man than I was to you?" he asked, completely ignoring my question.

"You wasn't a man at the time, Eugene," I answered. "Not yet, you wasn't," I added to smooth the blunt edge of my response.

He looked down at the table. "So I didn't do n-n-nothing wrong?" he asked.

I felt like I was talking to a child and wanted nothing more than for the conversation to be over. "No Eugene, you didn't do anything wrong. I was young myself and confused on top of that."

He nodded. "Well, I g-g-guess I better be getting on up the road. S'posed to rain later today."

Thank God. "Well, I enjoyed your company. I'm leaving tomorrow morning. So, let me gone get my hug now." I stood up to meet him at the door. We hugged and then he dug into his back pocket and handed me two one-hundred-dollar bills.

"What's this for?" I asked, pretending to be genuinely confused.

"I'm g-g-giving you your money back."

"It's not mine."

"Ain't n-n-nobody else around here got this kind of money. S-s-soon as I saw you in them fancy night clothes, I knowed that it was you who'd left it. Now unless you want me driving in the rain, then I suggest you take it b-b-because I ain't leaving 'til you do."

I smiled, shook my head, and took the money. I admired that about him and a part of me wished that I'd done right by him. He deserved it. The other part of me knew better than to go thinking those kinds of thoughts. What's done is done. Ain't no sense in looking back and it damn sure ain't no sense in trying to work him into my future. Plus, he wouldn't want nothing to do with me and my five kids anyway. Then, the voice returned:

What happens to your daughters has everything to do with you.

I didn't feel like going back down that lane. All I wanted was a little rest and relaxation after having a nice bath and a good breakfast. Plus, I'd done some good by apologizing to Eugene for the pain that I'd caused him.

No you didn't.

"I did too," I said and then thought back on the conversation and realized that I didn't. "Either way, he should be over it by now. Shit, he grown."

But your daughters aren't.

"You don't think I know that?" I yelled back. I was losing my mind. I grabbed the jug of white lightening from the freezer and poured myself a glass. I finished it one gulp and then poured another. I needed enough poison in my system so that I could forget. The only thing that I wanted to do was exist. No thoughts or memories were necessary. I reminded myself that I would be back in New Orleans with too much to do to think in less than 24 hours.

After the third glass, I passed right on out. By the time that I woke up, I was no longer home alone. Etta had made her way back over and was cleaning out our mama's closet.

"Girl, you have got to stop drinking like that. You gon' find yourself in the hospital one of these days."

I had a slight headache and was in no mood to argue. "Bring me an aspirin."

She shook her head. "About as bad as the man that I call my husband," she mumbled under her breath.

"Where he at anyway? I've been here for damn near four weeks and have yet to meet him."

"Ain't no telling. I stopped asking. As long as the bills are paid, then I'm alright."

I remembered the feeling and I didn't miss it. That kind of love didn't feel good. It drained the life out of you and if you weren't careful, then you'd be running around and popping pills trying to maintain all the ailments he caused you. Whenever a woman preferred to be anywhere but home, then it was a problem.

She returned with two white pills and a glass of water. "Thank you," I said, choosing not to complain about there being no ice in my water.

"You welcome. So, you ready to gone back home?"

I shrugged. "Guess I don't have much of a choice. Houses can't take care of themselves."

"True, true," she said, nodding. "You ain't gotta answer if you don't want to, but I'm curious. Do your kids live in that whorehouse too?"

I laughed and shook my head. "No, they don't. They stay far away actually. Why don't you have any?" I asked.

She took a deep breath. "Can't have none," she answered.

"I'm sorry."

"It's okay. Not like it's your fault."

The dreaded silence had crept into the room. It made me feel bad. It made me feel like even worse of a mother. It told me that I should be ashamed of myself; reminded me of how I felt cursed each time that I got pregnant; repeated that my twin sister would never have any children of her own. It made sure that I knew, without a shadow of a doubt, that I was wrong.

I needed a reminder. I knew that I was wrong. Sometimes I wished for denial. Those in denial live with no regrets or shame. As long as the finger is pointed elsewhere, they feel secure in the skin that they're in. After all, it's not their fault. But those like me, those that know better, live in hell. And, let the church folk tell it, then when we die we'll go right back to living in hell.

I knew that I should've at least attempted to right my wrongs. I could've opened up to Etta and I'm sure that she would've helped me, but I couldn't. My pride wouldn't let me. It went from my shield to being my prison and real joy can't exist behind bars. Trust me, I've been there.

"What you gon' do with Mama clothes?" I asked.

"Since neither one of us can fit 'em, I guess I'll take 'em to the Salvation Army up in Natchitoches."

"Oh. I went to her grave yesterday."

She nodded. "Did you get what you were looking for?"

I shrugged. "I don't know. I don't even know why I took my butt up there."

"In due time."

"I know," I sighed. "It still bothers me how you know what Mama's favorites were while I haven't a clue."

"I spent more time with Mama than you did."

"That wasn't all by my choice. I remember when you and Mama would haul off and go to the store and leave me home alone for hours. Or, what about the time that she said that y'all were going to the store real quick and ended up going to Shreveport?"

"Louisa, Shreveport around the corner. That ain't nowhere. Plus, you said that you didn't care."

"You were teasing me. I had to pretend not to care, but you knew that I was lying. I hated this city! Anywhere, besides here, was somewhere."

"Well, on behalf of our mama, allow me to apologize."

"Don't. Just pretend that I never even said anything about it."

"I don't try to take up for Mama, Louisa. I really—"

"Yes, you do," I cut in.

"Okay, well maybe I do. You're right. I did spend more time with her than you did. That's why I know that she had demons of her to deal with. She wasn't perfect, just like you ain't perfect, I ain't perfect, and Maman wasn't perfect."

"Don't go bringing Maman into this."

"Why wouldn't I? She had a lot to do with the way that Mama was. She didn't raise her, you know? She ran off with some man and left Mama in an orphanage. She came back, trying to apologize, but it was too late. Mama was grown, had kids of her own, and wasn't trying to hear nothing Maman had to say."

"Well, if she hated her own mama so much, then why did she always send me over there to be with her? You were hardly ever there."

She shrugged. "I can't answer that, but at the same time, I remember being jealous of you for that. You would come home with all kinds of knickknacks. She never got me anything."

"You didn't need anything! Mama bought you everything!" I screamed.

"What you want me to say, Louisa?"

I didn't have an answer. "I'm sorry."

"Don't be. I understand how you feel and I wish that I had all the answers for you, but I don't."

"I know."

"Now, I'm only telling you this because I love you. You need to find a god. I ain't qualified to tell nobody which one to pick, but you need to find one. Jesus works for me, but it's a whole slew of religions out there. I read in one book that some people think God is a woman."

I cocked my head to the side, interested. "Really?" I asked.

"Hey, if they like it then I love it. Religion ain't nothing but a tool to help get you through life without killing yourself or anybody else. That's all it is and is exactly why you need to find one before alcohol becomes the death of you."

"Well until I find one, I'll keep right on sipping."

She laughed which caused me to laugh. We kept on cackling like two fools until we had aching stomachs and tears in our eyes. The past few weeks had been good for us. We'd done our fair share of arguing, but our making up is what mattered most. It may have taken more than twenty years, but I'd finally gotten my sister back.

I now had someone to call that was worth calling. I knew that someone cared about me. Someone would be checking up on me and maybe even visiting me. And if I disappeared from the face of the earth, someone wasn't going to rest until I was found.

Instead of going home that night, Etta stayed over with me. We slept in the same room that we'd grown up in together. We sang, danced, joked, and laughed like ten-year-old girls that had the house to themselves until we passed out.

When we woke, we had breakfast and shared the paper. Afterwards, we sat out on the porch discussing the news up until my driver pulled up to take me back to New Orleans. We hugged as if it was our last time and I prayed to God that it wouldn't be. We said our goodbyes and made our promises to keep in touch.

Chapter 17

T hat same night found me back on the porch with a cup of feel
good. Only this time, I was at 1026 Conti Street in New
Orleans, Louisiana. I had two thousand dollars to my name
and the only reason that I had that was because it was hidden in a
sock. When I get to hell, I'll have to remember to thank Walter for
the sock trick. Not even the police department caught on.

The girls were all gone and the only company that I had was a
letter from Jacquelyn and the bearer of the all the bad news—
Andrew Rousseau. He worked for the Times Picayune and had
been begging to interview me. He wanted to write a book on the
evolution of Storyville, which was thought to be disbanded over
60 years ago. It never left. It dispersed and was passed down from
generation to generation. From one queen—Norma Wallace, to
another—Josephine DuBois. I'd been brushing the child off for the
past few months, but on that night, I told him just about whatever
it was that he wanted to know.

"How old are you?" he asked.

"35."

"How did you get started in this business?"

I decided to have a little fun with that answer. You know, just
in case I wound up in a history book or something. "Well, I was
tired of men telling women what they could and couldn't do with
their bodies. Men, well white men, determine if women can leave

the house, file for divorce, work, vote, take birth control, get an abortion. They can prostitute, now they can't, now they can, and now they can't. The state might as well have a remote control on us." I laughed. "I wanted to give women a safe space to do whatever it was that their hearts desired to do."

"Are you a lesbian?" He looked up at me. I cracked up laughing. "You don't have to answer that if you don't want to. I can just ask another question."

"No, it's okay. No, I'm not a lesbian. I was actually married once before."

His eyebrows shot up. "To who?"

"His name was Trouble Man."

"Was that his real name?"

I nodded my head.

"What happened? Did you all get a divorce?"

"I killed him."

He stopped writing, but never looked up. "How did you do it?" he asked carefully.

"With my best cast iron pot."

"Okay. Umm, umm…Where you from?"

"From a lil' old country town."

"What's the name of it?"

"Lil' old country town."

"Okay. What's your real name?" he asked.

"Josephine," I answered.

"Well, I ask because when you were arrested, I looked up Josephine DuBois, but none was there."

"You must have checked the wrong jail."

"No, it was the right one. Orleans Parish. To be sure, I checked the surrounding parishes too. I even—"

"I said you must have checked the wrong jail."

He nodded his head. "Yes ma'am. I'm sorry. Okay, what was your connection to Norma Wallace?"

"None at all. I didn't even know her."

"But she gave you her house."

I shrugged. "And I thank her for it, but your guess is as good as mine. She admired me is what the lawyer said."

He cocked his head to the side. "I can see that."

He scribbled a few more lines in his little notebook and then added that he just had a few more questions before he was on his way. Some I answered and some I didn't. Some I told the truth on and others I lied. The last question is the one that damn near threw me off my rocker.

"I hope this doesn't upset you, but I waited a good while for you to come back. And umm, while I waited, I read the letter."

"I got a good mind to knock you clean upside your head for going through my shit, but go on."

"Well uh, Jacquelyn mentioned that you were giving someone named Freckles money to give to your children. She said that Freckles had long since stopped delivering the money, but well, what I want to know is what your relationship is with your children. How many do you have? And, if you don't mind my asking, where are they and why aren't you, you know? With your kids."

"Get the fuck off my property."

"You don't have to answer that. I'm sorry. Let's move on to the closing statements. What—"

"I said leave!" I screamed, standing to my feet.

He stood and began backing off of the porch slowly. "What's your association with Earl Banks?"

I opened the front door and went straight to the back for my gun. I expected him to be gone, but when I came back, he was standing in the street, right in front of the house. He looked down at the gun in my hand and back up at me. "Did he father your children? Did you cheat on your husband with him?"

I wasn't crazy enough to kill a white boy in the middle of the street, but I was crazy enough to make him think I would. I raised my arm straight up in the air and pulled the trigger. That finally got his feet moving faster. He pushed his hat down on his head and hauled ass. Seconds later, he pulled off in a little white raggedy car. I went back in the house, tucked my gun away, and poured myself a second round. After I'd emptied half of the cup, I pulled out Jacquelyn's letter to read it.

Dear Josephine,

It is with great sadness that I write this letter. The morning after you departed, we were raided. It was truly a savage sight to see. They turned over everything and handled our possessions as if they held no value. They treated us like criminals, pressing us for answers. They said that we would be jailed if we didn't cooperate on charges of obstruction. So, we told. We thought it safe since you were away. That meant that we would all maintain our freedom.

It was my belief that we would reunite and begin anew, but you always said that I could be a dingbat. The twins made away with all of your clothes and jewelry. I have no clue if they went North, South, East, or West. I overheard Freckles on the phone mentioning that she had been saving all of the money that she was supposed to be delivering to your children. She's gone to California.

I didn't know that you had children. They're beautiful, I'm sure. Paulette is with me. We're safe and after some talking,

*we decided to begin a new chapter. No more whoring for us.
We're trying for acting instead. Hopefully that does not anger
you, but makes you proud. Your strength will forever be my
inspiration.*

*There were three cigars left. I took two for myself and
Paulette. It's the only thing I took, I swear. When you smoke
it, think of us as we'll be thinking of you. Thanks for
everything.*

Love,

Jacquelyn

I refolded the letter and put it back in its envelope. I had no
time to cry over what I should've, could've, or would've done.
Decisions needed to be made. I had an even two thousand dollars
to my name and the house that I was sitting in, which had been
willed to me, was soon to be mine, no longer. It had been
"forfeited" just as my last one was. According to Charlotte, my
attorney, under federal and state laws, law enforcement has a right
to seize property if it is used to commit a crime or was purchased
with money earned from criminal activity. I asked if I would be
repaid since the house was worth almost a quarter million dollars.
I wasn't surprised when she shook her head no.

That left me with three options. Well, two really, because if
Freckles was keeping the money and if they hadn't been evicted
yet, then that means somebody was paying bills. Whether they
were sleeping around to get the money or working for it doesn't
take away from the fact that it was getting done. The rent was
being paid. Doris was the woman of that house and there was no
way in hell they would let me back in.

I could've gone back to renting and found myself an honest
job, but who was I fooling? There wasn't no way, in this lifetime,
that I was going to work for somebody else and pay somebody

else's mortgage. That's like turning your freedom papers back in to be a slave again. No thanks. I'd rather find a new house with the little money that I did have to my name, pick up more girls, and start all over. But truth be told, I was tired. Thirty five years of living, but it felt like I'd lived it twice. *I was tired.*

My chin was resting on my chest and my eyes had sealed themselves shut. I dreamed of dark clouds, heavy rain, strong winds, and...bullfrogs singing. *Bullfrogs sing when rain is coming.* I tried to run home, but there was none. The bullfrogs were getting louder and louder. I gave up and decided to run to Coushatta. It was far away, but I could see it up ahead. It was sunny there: no rain, no winds, and no bullfrogs.

Before I made it there, I was woken up by the chime of the doorbell ringing. It took me a lazy minute to realize that the doorbell was actually ringing and I wasn't just dreaming. I asked who it was. I heard a woman's voice, but couldn't make out what she was saying. It had really started raining. Pouring too. To be on the safe side, I grabbed my gun before answering the door. I saw who it was and liked to shot myself in the foot.

"Is it a bad time?" Jewel asked.

I didn't answer her. I closed the door, took the top lock off, and opened the door for her to come in. She lowered her umbrella, shook it, and leaned it against the wall. She took a deep breath while looking around as a child would, shamelessly. She ran her hands up and down her arms and I offered her a cup of coffee.

"I'll take something stronger if you have it."

My face must have asked what my mouth didn't. I've always been pretty bad at hiding how I felt.

"Yes, I drink now. Hollywood will do it to you."

I poured the last bit of scotch that I had left between both of our glasses. I handed her one and then sat on the sofa across from the one that she sat on. She took a sip and her shoulders relaxed.

The way she was acting, you would've thought that I was her landlord and she was getting herself ready to explain why she didn't have my money.

"So what brought you this way?" I asked, getting straight to the point.

"Well, it's been a while."

"And?"

"And I missed you, Louisa. I missed our friendship. You were like a sister to me."

"Is that right?" I took a sip. I knew that I would have a hangover something serious the next morning, but I would have to deal with that when the time came.

"Look, I know that I don't exactly deserve the award for best friend of the year, but I had to do what I had to do and if anyone else can understand that then it should be you."

"You telling me about myself or asking me?" I asked.

"I'm telling you, Louisa."

"It's Josephine," I corrected her.

"To them—" she said, pointing to the door, "—it's Josephine, but you'll always be Louisa to me."

"Well, why don't we just have us a family reunion? Excuse me while I go grab the fried chicken and potato salad. Afterwards, we can hug and kiss and pretend like nothing ever went wrong. Like you didn't turn me and my kids down when we ain't had nowhere else to go in the name of shaking your ass in front of a crowd of white folk and expect me to understand."

She put her drink down and sat up. "You damn right I expect you to understand. Just like I understood when you left them girls of yours to fend for themselves while you went out to make a better life for yourself. You don't think I heard? The streets talk, Louisa."

"It's Josephine."

"It's Louisa," she said, standing her ground.

"It's Josephine and what happens between me and my kids ain't got a damn thing to do with you."

"No, but the hundred dollar bill that I put in Doris' hand had everything to do with me. The damn kids were starving. She was standing on the corner to…well, you know what. And I—"

"And you were a damn fool to believe that I just up and left them high and dry. Not only did I leave them with money, but I sent money by every week. If she was on the corner, then dammit it's because she wanted to be there." It wasn't the whole truth, but I wasn't just about to let her talk to me any old kind of way.

"I don't doubt you. I just thought that you should know."

"Well, I thank you Miss Jewel. May God bless your kind white soul for coming out of your Hollywood way to feed the poor little black kids."

"You can be such a bitch."

"I learn from the best," I replied.

She shook her head and cracked the tiniest smile. It must have been contagious because before I knew it, I'd started smiling too and then we were up looking like fools, laughing and crying in the middle of a near-dark, living room.

"Turn on the air conditioner or something. I'm burning up," she said, fanning herself.

"Ain't none. You ain't noticed that the only lights we have is them candles up there? Police ransacked the place and claimed it as their own."

"Get out of here."

"I'm serious."

"How can they do that? They shouldn't be able to do that. I have an attorney. I'll help you. We have to fight this. I get so sick of—"

"Drop it. I have an attorney too and *trust me*, they can and they did."

"Well what are you going to do now?"

"Move on back to Coushatta."

"You swore that you would never go back."

"I don't know about you, but I've learned that the older you get, the list of things you say that you'll never do tends to get shorter and shorter," I said, chuckling. "Come on, let's go outside. It is a bit warm in here and I heard that white folk melt in the heat."

"Hahaha."

"That ain't true?" I asked sarcastically.

We went out to the porch, all out in the open like I had a right to be there. Since there were no chairs, we sat on the top step. The air was heavy and I just knew that my curls were shot to shit, but it didn't matter. I didn't have a person left to impress and there wasn't much impressing left in my bones—if any at all. I decided right there on the porch, in the confinement of my skull, that I was going to go with the flow from that point on. At that moment, the flow consisted of being on the porch, waiting on the next breeze while comparing about the then and the now. We had a good time too; we laughed, cried, and of course, we did some fussing. It was like old times before either of us had made a name for ourselves.

"So you're really done for good?" she asked.

Instead of opening my mouth, I just nodded my head.

"Well how was it being a madam?"

I shrugged. "It had its ups and downs."

It was her turn to nod her head.

"How is it being an actress and living in Hollywood?" I asked.

"Being an actress has its ups and downs. I'm nothing more than a well-paid whore. They tell me what to say, how to say it, where to say it, when to say it, and how much I'll get for saying it." She chuckled. "And never could I live in Hollywood. It's stressful enough working there. If they want me to work, then they have to fly me in."

"Don't sound that bad to me. So where do you live?"

"Right there in Algier's Point," she said, pointing toward the Mississippi River which divided her side of town from mine.

Again, I just nodded. I wanted to ask why she hadn't come sooner if she lived so close. The answer wouldn't have changed anything though, so I just kept the question to myself. At the same time, I wanted to congratulate her since she'd long since wanted to live in Algiers. But I didn't say that either. I just left it as a thought. It was my guess that she was holding back words of her own, because for a while, it was quieter than a graveyard. That meant that we'd reached that point in the visit where we both knew that it had reached its ending. As the host, it was only polite of me to wait for her to make the call.

Then it came. She yawned and looked down at her watch which happened to be pure gold, damn near heavier than her whole arm, and *very* expensive. I knew because I had one, though I was pretty damn sure that if the police didn't get it, then the twins got it. I bought mine after overhearing so many men brag on it. They called it The Oyster and it was supposed to be the first watch to have quartz movement, whatever that meant. I just knew that I had to have it; I got off on having things that men wished for and it all started with the convertible that Earl bought for me. Men used to damn near break their necks trying to get a look at my car. I had the car, the jewelry, the women, and I smoked cigars. No wonder they made it their mission to shut my ass down.

"Well, I better be getting on 'cross this river," she said, yawning again.

"Alrighty," I answered, having to yawn too, all of a sudden.

She stood up and stretched, in the very same way that my sister did after leaving me on our mama's porch. Etta had left to return to her dream which resided across the tracks. Now, Jewel was returning to hers, across the river to Algiers Point. She got her chance to work down at The 500 Club, starred in movies, and got to be known by just about everybody on this side of the planet. That's exactly what she wanted for herself. She had to leave plenty behind to get it, but she got it. Ain't that what matters most?

To me, it is. I wanted out of Coushatta. I wanted bigger and better. I was tired of being told no so I wanted to create a life for myself where I wouldn't have to ask. Instead, they would have to ask me. I would have the freedom to come and go; to not want for long; to be able to say "you're welcome" versus "please."

I didn't just sit on top of my want either. I went out and got that for myself. I took all of the shit that life threw at me, smoothed it down real nice, and built a life on it. That life took me from where I was to where I wanted to be and I prided myself on that. Not many people had the courage to do it. It's one hell of chorus out there singing about their children making something of themselves since they never could. Getting across is the dream of many, but the reality of few.

Epilogue

"So did you ever talk to Jewel again?"

"Nope, but I think we both knew that our night on the porch was the last time. What's your name again, baby?"

"Monica," the young nurse answered.

"Monica," I repeated. "I like that."

"Thank you. Now, let's get back to the story. You ain't finish telling me. So, what your sister say when you moved back home?"

"What could she say?" I asked. "I was back and that's all there was to it."

"See, that's why I like you Ms. Louisa. Or do you want me to call you Ms. Josephine?"

"Don't matter to me none."

"So if all you had was two grand and you ain't work no more, then how can you afford to stay here? Shoot, this place ain't cheap."

I chuckled. "Just like how I told you my story. Everybody else wanna hear it too. So much that they be willing to pay me for it."

"How much, Ms. Louisa?"

"Don't worry about that. Just know it's enough to keep me going."

"So they still pay you for the same story? I don't get it."

"That's 'cause you making it more complicated than what it is. You know damn well ain't nobody about to pay for something that they can read in the paper. I gives 'em a different story every time, me. I keep 'em guessing. I'm like the stories. It's something new with me every day."

She laughed, shaking her head. "Well I better go check on my other patients. You need something before I go?"

I shook my head. "Not for me, but bring Eugene a bag of them Chee-Wees back. He like 'em," I said, looking over at him. He just sat there in his chair smiling at me, looking just as dumb as the day we got caught in the barn together.

"Now you know he ain't supposed to be eating that."

"Girl, if you don't bring them damn chips I know something…"

She laughed. "Excuse me. I'll get your man the chips. I don't need you shooting at me or chasing me with no baseball bat."

She left out of the room and closed the door behind her. Eugene cleared his throat to get ready to say something. "You mi-i-i-ght wanna tell your d-d-daughters your story. I'm shh-ure they'd love to hear it."

"Child, them girls ain't caring nothing 'bout my life. They got they own tales to tell."